"You don't approve of me, do you."

"No, I don't." Oliver's words were blunt. "I don't approve of women like you, who were raised in the lap of luxury and swan through life thinking that hard work is something best left alone."

That stung, but Francesca didn't say anything.

"But so long as you do your job competently we'll get along just fine. Abuse your position and you'll soon discover the limits to my tolerance...."

CATHY WILLIAMS is Trinidadian and was brought up on the twin islands of Trinidad and Tobago. She was awarded a scholarship to study in Britain, and went to Exeter University in 1975 to continue her studies into the great loves of her life: languages and literature. It was there that Cathy met her husband, Richard. Since they married, Cathy has lived in England, originally in the Thames Valley but now in the Midlands. Cathy and Richard have three small daughters.

Books by Cathy Williams

HARLEQUIN PRESENTS®
1993—A DAUGHTER FOR CHRISTMAS
2006—A SUITABLE MISTRESS
2048—THE BABY VERDICT
2076—A NATURAL MOTHER

Don't miss any of our special offers. Write to us at the following address for information on our newest releases.

Harlequin Reader Service
U.S.: 3010 Walden Ave., P.O. Box 1325, Buffalo, NY 14269
Canadian: P.O. Box 609, Fort Erie, Ont. L2A 5X3

Cathy Williams

TO TAME A PROUD HEART

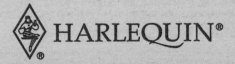

TORONTO • NEW YORK • LONDON
AMSTERDAM • PARIS • SYDNEY • HAMBURG
STOCKHOLM • ATHENS • TOKYO • MILAN • MADRID
PRAGUE • WARSAW • BUDAPEST • AUCKLAND

ISBN 0-373-12105-9

TO TAME A PROUD HEART

First North American Publication 2000.

Copyright © 1996 by Cathy Williams.

Visit us at www.eHarlequin.com

Printed in U.S.A.

CHAPTER ONE

FRANCESCA WADE was not a person given to nerves. She had the resilient self-confidence which came naturally to those who were good-looking or wealthy. In her case, both.

Right now, though, with her eyes dutifully glued to Kemp International's promotional magazine on her lap, she was feeling decidedly tense. She might have impulsively made the decision to come here, but she was discovering fast that this was the last place she wanted to be, and the temptation to take flight was enormous.

She kept reading, glancing covertly at her watch every so often, wondering where the hell The Man was. She had been shown into his outside office forty minutes previously, had smilingly been informed that Mr Kemp would be with her shortly, and here had she sat since. Waiting.

When the door opened she glanced up hopefully, and tried to wipe the growing resentment off her face.

'Mr Kemp will see you now.' It was the same smiling face that had ushered her into the office—neat grey little bun caught at the nape of her neck, navy blue suit, plumpish figure. She stood aside and Francesca made an effort to smile pleasantly back as she was led along the corridor to an intimidating mahogany door.

Suddenly the nerves gave way to something else—something more like alarm—and Francesca's mouth was dry as the door was pushed open.

The stylish designer suit which she had plucked from the wardrobe and donned because she thought that it conveyed the right image of businesslike efficiency now felt starched and uncomfortable. She was not accustomed to being so carefully dressed. She preferred casual clothes. She nervously smoothed down the skirt and looked around her, her eyes settling on the figure in the chair, his back towards her.

Behind her the door closed deferentially, and the figure in the chair swung around.

What had she expected? She realised that she had no idea—vague impressions, yes. She had spent weeks listening to her father's well-placed insinuations that it was time she found herself a job, that she couldn't sit back and indulge in useless creature comforts for ever, to him telling her that he knew someone—the son of a friend of his, a charming fellow.

It had been a quiet game of gradual persuasion, aimed at eroding her objections—the age-old water-dripping-on-a-stone technique—so that now, standing here, she found that she could hardly recall any recent conversation with her father which hadn't been vaguely permeated with descriptions of the wretched Oliver Kemp.

'He's a self-made man,' her father had told her in his early, enthusiastic phase, before her constant, stubborn refusals to have her life sorted out for her had obliged him to take a more subtle stance. 'Grabbed the proverbial bootlaces and hauled himself up, inch by inch, until now he's worth millions.'

That had conjured up images of a sour-faced young man grappling up the face of a cliff, growing ever fatter on the way as he made money and did all those wonderful things which had clearly awed her father.

The man facing her was not fat. Nor was he sour-faced. He had a disturbing brand of good looks—the sort of good looks which she had never before encountered among her young rich set. Every feature was strong and aggressive and his light blue eyes were mesmerising, hypnotic.

He stared at her openly, not blinking, until she lowered her eyes. 'Sit,' he commanded—a coldly uttered monosyllable that made her flinch.

He gave no apologies for having kept her waiting, but then he didn't strike her as the sort of man who went in much for apologising. Probably, she thought, he didn't even know how to spell the word.

She sat down opposite him, across the gleaming boardroom table, at one end of which was a word processor and several sheets of paper.

'How did you hear of this job?' he asked bluntly. 'It wasn't nationally advertised.'

'From my father,' Francesca confessed reluctantly, already on the defensive for reasons which she couldn't even identify.

'Ah, yes.' He stared at her, and she thought irritably, What does *that* mean?

'He mentioned that you were a friend of his and that you were looking for a secretary.' She was even more irritated to find herself rushing into a little explanatory speech. 'He thought that I might be interested.'

'I had lunch with your father weeks ago,' Oliver informed her coolly. 'How is it, if you're that interested in finding work, that you've only now decided to come here for an interview?'

Interview? she wanted to ask. What interview? This was more like a cross-examination. What exactly was she *guilty* of? she wondered.

'Unless, of course, you've been busy going to other interviews?'

He let the question hang in the air challengingly, while he continued to look at her with coolly polite indifference.

'Not as such,' Francesca admitted, disliking him more with each passing minute.

'*Not as such*? What does "not as such" mean? Either you've been going to interviews or you haven't.'

'This is the first,' she muttered, trying to comfort herself with the thought that she didn't really want this job anyway, that she had been goaded into it by her father.

'And how long is it since you left college?' He appeared smilingly vague. Did he, she wondered, think that she had been born yesterday? He would know exactly how long it was since she had left college because her father would have told him.

'Several months.'

'So, if you haven't been working or even, as you tell me, looking for a job, what were you doing for "several months"? Resting?'

'Look, Mr Kemp,' she said, through gritted teeth, 'I came here for an interview. All these questions you're asking me aren't relevant to whether or not I'm capable of doing the job, are they?'

'Miss Wade—' he leaned forward and there was a soft, cold threat in his voice '—you don't decide what's relevant or what's not. I do. If you don't like it, then the door is right behind you.' He stared at her, and for a split second she was seriously tempted to leave, but strangely she didn't want to be browbeaten by this man.

'So,' he said with the same unsettling softness in his voice, 'are we going to continue?'

She nodded. There really was something very threatening about this man, she thought. It sat on his shoulders like an invisible cloak.

'Shall I tell you why you haven't bothered to stir yourself into getting a job sooner, Miss Wade?' he asked with pointed casualness. 'Your father is a rich man, and rich girls have no need for jobs. No doubt jobs get in the way of late nights, partying, men—'

Francesca's head shot up at that one. 'That's an insult, Mr Kemp!' she snapped. 'You have no right to make assumptions about my character!'

He shrugged negligently and stood up. She watched him as he strolled across to the window, one hand casually thrust into his trouser pocket, his face half turned away as he idly surveyed the scene outside.

There was a panther-like grace about him. His body was lean, muscular, as much of a threat as his dark good looks. All in all, she didn't like him—about as much as he didn't like her. He had no intention of employing her, of course. No doubt the only reason he had agreed to see her in the first place was because he vaguely knew her father. She should never have let herself be emotionally railroaded into this.

'You need to settle down,' her father had told her the evening before. 'You're a bright girl—too bright for a life of constant parties and holidays and shopping.'

For the first time she had sensed a certain amount of irritated despair in him. There had been no gentle teasing in his voice, none of the sly nagging in which he took great amusement.

He was right, she had thought reluctantly. She had left her expensive private school at eighteen, with three A levels under her belt, had sailed through a very expensive secretarial course, which she had taken simply because she couldn't face the thought of going to university, and ever since then had done very little about finding a job.

She frowned at the image her mind threw up of herself—too rich, too pretty, content to drift along with her crowd of friends who appeared to fritter their lives away happily doing nothing in particular, or else indulging in

sporadic bursts of fruitful energy when they would do a
course on photography or cordon bleu cookery, or anything else that enjoyably absorbed a bit time but didn't
inconveniently leave an aftertaste for something more.

She wasn't like that. She knew that. But if she wasn't
why had she allowed herself to flow with the tide instead
of taking her life in her own two hands?

Oliver Kemp had turned to face her. His back was to
the window now, and the harsh, winter sun threw his face
into angular shadows.

'The fact is, Miss Wade, that I don't know precisely
what your motives are in coming here, but if the only
reason is to get your father off your back then you've come
to the wrong place.'

He hadn't smiled once, she realised, since she had
walked into this office.

'Of course that's not the reason why I'm here—' she
began, reddening because there was too much truth in his
observation for comfort, and he cut in abruptly.

'Really?' The ice-blue eyes raked over her thoroughly,
and clearly disapproved of what they saw.

'I apologise for taking up your time, Mr Kemp,'
Francesca said stiffly, standing up. 'But I'm afraid I made
a mistake in coming here; I'm afraid that I can't accept
any job you have to offer.'

'Sit back down, Miss Wade, and kindly do not think
about leaving until I am through with you.'

'I have no intention of sitting back down, Mr Kemp,'
she replied equally coldly, 'and kindly do not patronise me
by treating me like a child.'

'I wouldn't,' he said smoothly, 'if you would start acting
like an adult. Your father mentioned that you needed to
settle down, that he was at his wits' end with you. God
only knows what sorts of high jinks you've been getting

up to, but I can well imagine. The fact is that I don't really give a damn what you do or don't do in your personal time, but my company isn't a rehabilitation clinic and I'm not in the business of setting wayward children back on the straight and narrow.'

Francesca actually only managed to absorb part of this. Her mind seemed to shut off when he got to 'high jinks', and anger flooded through her like a crashing tidal wave.

'I am not,' she managed to splutter, 'some kind of charity case, Mr Kemp. I was not obliged to come here and you are certainly not obliged to give me this job!'

'No,' he agreed, but his expression was shuttered.

'And for your information I am not a wayward child!'

'Really?' Mild disbelief bordered on downright indifference, but he wasn't about to let her put her point across. He pointed to the word processor on the table.

'Let's dispense with the histrionics,' he said coolly, making her sound, she thought furiously, like a candidate for the local mental asylum. 'I might as well find out if you're qualified for the job anyway. I want you to type the document at the side of the computer, and then I'll dictate some letters to you.

'Your father said that your secretarial skills were excellent but—' he looked at her with enough disbelief to make her teeth snap together in anger '—whether that was paternal pride talking is left to be seen.'

Francesca smiled sweetly at him and rose to go over to the terminal. 'Indeed,' she said. This at any rate was one area in which she was supremely confident. 'And, forgetting paternal pride,' she said, sitting down and quickly switching on the machine, 'anything I learnt at secretarial school might well have been forgotten after six months of partying, late nights and—what was it? Oh, yes—men. *And* high jinks and debauchery. Wouldn't you agree?'

She threw him another sweet smile. He didn't smile back at her, but there was a sudden shift in his expression, and she glimpsed behind the powerful, aggressive face a suggestion of charm that was an unnerving as his insolence had been.

She looked away quickly and began typing, her fingers flying smoothly over the keyboard. She could feel Oliver Kemp watching her, perched on the edge of the boardroom table, one hand resting lightly on his thigh—watching and waiting for her to sink obligingly to the level of his preconceived notions of her.

She glared at the word processer. True, she had come here of her own accord; true, her father, although he hadn't actually arranged the interview himself had hinted long and hard enough. He had also caught her at her weakest moment.

She frowned, and wondered whether she would be sitting here now if she had not spent that one misguided night with Rupert a few days before. Dear Rupert—tall, blond, carefree, with more money than sense most of the time. Her father thoroughly disapproved of him, and when he had discovered her whereabouts he had hit the proverbial roof. It had made not the slightest difference that Rupert Thompson held about as much sexual allure for her as a baked potato.

Her eyes slid across to where Oliver was sitting. If her father absolutely had to interfere, she thought, the least he could have done would have been to recommend her to someone halfway human—someone easygoing and amiable. Oliver Kemp, she decided, was as easygoing and amiable as a cyclone.

She printed the five pages of typed document and handed them to him with a blankly polite expression.

The cold blue eyes skimmed over them, then he read

them more slowly. Checking for errors, she thought. No doubt hoping for them. If any existed he could go back to her father with a rueful shake of his head and say, in all truth, that she just had not got the necessary skills to work for him, but that he would keep his ear to the ground as a favour to him.

Maybe, she thought suddenly, I should have inserted enough mistakes to have guaranteed that rueful shake of the head. But her only thought at the time had been to show the damned man that she wasn't the completely frivolous nitwit that he obviously thought she was. Shame. The best ideas, like the best retorts, always came to mind after the event.

'Not bad.' He deposited the sheets of typed paper next to him and walked across to the door, expecting her to follow, which she did, brushing past him then following him towards the office where she had sat for forty minutes earlier.

His own office was through the connecting door. It was huge, with two desks, one of which was his, the other housing a computer terminal and printer. Extending along one side of the room was a floor-to-ceiling bookcase, handmade in the same rich dark wood as the rest of the furniture, with rows of books on electronics.

Kemp International had cornered the market in sophisticated electronic equipment, and had always managed to stay one step ahead of its rivals.

Francesca eyed the books and wondered whether this was Oliver Kemp's personal taste in literature as well. Was he one of those men who ate, slept and dreamt work?

'I would expect you to be au fait,' he said, following the direction of her eyes, 'with the contents of most of the books on those shelves. Working for me isn't simply a question of being an adequate typist.'

'So you've decided that I'm good enough for the job, Mr Kemp?' she asked, with an expression of surprise. She didn't know whether to be astounded or dismayed by this. 'Does this mean that you don't think my father's verbal curriculum vitae was based entirely on paternal pride?'

He sat back in his swivel chair and linked his fingers together. 'Sarcasm is not a trait I admire in a secretary,' he drawled.

Oh, dear, oh, dear, oh, dear, Francesca felt like saying; then we might as well call this a day, mightn't we? But she swallowed down the rejoinder. Her father would be elated that she had taken him up on his suggestion, that she had landed this job through her own skills in the end, and she dearly loved him.

'I do apologise,' she murmured, and he frowned at her.

'You've proved,' he said, giving her reply the benefit of the doubt, 'that you can type.'

'And that I can read,' she pointed out. 'I shall consume the contents of those books avidly.'

His eyebrows flew up at that, and she hurriedly began stammering out a suitable apology.

He waited patiently until her voice had fizzled out into a series of fairly inaudible noises.

'Good. Because when clients call with queries you will have to respond to them in a coherent, knowledgeable fashion.'

He paused, and she said into the silence, 'What happened to your last secretary?'

'My last secretary,' he said lazily, 'emigrated to Australia to live with her daughter three years ago. Since then I've been subjected to a string of women ranging from the downright dim to the misplaced intellectual.'

So you wouldn't describe yourself as fussy? Francesca

wanted to ask. 'I see,' she said, only, in fact, seeing a series of hopeless confrontations ahead of her.

'You, at least, have started off in vaguely the right direction. You can spell at any rate.' He looked at her through his lashes, his face expressionless. 'Which brings me to the obvious question. Why are you here?'

'I thought you knew why I was here,' she answered, bewildered by the question. 'I'm a spoiled brat who—'

'Why are you *really* here?' he interrupted impatiently. 'What are you doing here when you could have got yourself a job at any number of companies if you'd wanted. Your father informed me that you had excellent A level results. Why didn't you go to university?'

Francesca looked at him resentfully, not liking the way he was manoeuvring her into a position of self-defence.

'Your father wanted you to go to university.'

'He did,' she agreed.

'He wanted you to study economics, I believe.'

'Did you talk about anything at this lunch of yours apart from me?' she asked with irritation. 'I suppose you also know what dress size I am, and what my favourite colour is as well?'

She hadn't expected a response to that, but he looked at her very carefully, his eyes roaming over her body and sending a reeling sensation of alarm through her. Men had looked at her before—in fact she was quite used to interested stares—but she had never felt this nervous prickle down her spine.

'Size eight, and, with your hair, probably green—dark green.'

'I didn't go to university,' she said hurriedly, flushing, 'because I wanted a break from studying.'

'A break to do what?'

'To enjoy myself,' she muttered feebly, feeling like a cornered rat.

'Ah, now we're getting to the heart of the matter, aren't we?'

'Are we?' she asked, already feeling her hackles beginning to rise.

'You may have all the qualifications for this job, and God only knows I've seen more than enough internal applications by way of comparison, but don't for a minute imagine that I shall tolerate your personal life spilling over into your professional one. Working for me isn't going to be a game to be endured simply to humour your father. I don't want to see you enter this office either late or the worse for all-night partying. Do I make myself clear?'

'As a bell,' she said coldly.

'Nor do I expect you to spend your time rushing through your work so that you can get on the telephone to your numerous admirers.'

'I don't have numerous admirers, Mr Kemp,' she snapped. 'And I can't believe that Dad would have told you that I did.'

He shrugged. 'He mentioned some playboy who was always in tow, and playboys tend to travel in packs, don't they? They don't feel complete unless they're enjoying their wild times in the company of like-minded individuals.' There was contempt on his face.

'You don't approve of me, do you, Mr Kemp?' she asked stiffly.

'No, I don't.' His words were blunt. He was not the sort of man to beat about the bush, nor was he the sort to parcel up unflattering thoughts underneath pretty wrapping.

'I grew up poor, Miss Wade, and I made it on my own. I don't approve of playboys who can't see further than having a good time. Nor do I approve of women like you, who were raised in the lap of luxury and swan through life thinking that hard work is something best left alone. You obviously have the brains to do something for yourself, but that doesn't appeal, does it? Hard work is rarely glamorous to those who don't have to do it.'

That stung. She felt angry hurt prick the back of her eyes but she didn't say anything. She could hardly deny that she had been indulged all her life, could she? By the time she had been born, late in her parents' lives, her father had already made his first million and had been well on his way to making several more.

Would things have been different if her mother had lived? Probably. But in the absence of a mother her father had spoilt her, doted on her, bought her everything that her heart had desired. There was so much, she later realised, that he had wanted to make up for—for the lack of a mother, for the long hours he worked and, most of all, it had been his way of showing her how much he loved her.

But maybe Oliver Kemp was right. Maybe showering her with material things had taken away from her that hungry edge that drove people on to succeed. She thought of her friends—all pampered, all the indulged products of wealthy parents, charming enough people to whom hardship was unknown and suffering was measured in terms of missed skiing holidays.

'But those are my personal feelings,' he said coolly, breaking into her introspection. 'Personal feelings have no place in a working environment, though. Just so long as you do your job competently then we'll get along just fine. Abuse your position, my girl, and you'll soon discover the limits to my tolerance.'

They stared at each other, and she felt panic rise up in

her throat. This was never going to work out. He disliked her and he disliked everything that she stood for.

'Thank you for making me feel so warmly welcomed into your organisation, Mr Kemp,' she said stiffly, and his lips curved into an unwilling smile which totally altered the forbidding angularity of his face.

He stood up to show her into her office. 'I see,' he murmured over his shoulder, their eyes meeting, 'that that biting tongue of yours might be something I shall *have* to tolerate. However,' he continued, turning away and walking into the outer office, 'there's no need to dress in designer clothes.'

He sat on the edge of her desk, waiting for her to sit down, then he leant towards her. 'I say this for your own benefit. The people with whom you'll be mixing don't come from such a rarefied background as you do.' He reached out to finger the lapel of her expensive shirt. 'Too much of this and you might find yourself distanced by a group of very nice people indeed.'

She didn't pull away from his touch, but she wanted to. Instead, as he strolled back into his office, she found that her body had become rigid, and she only began to relax as she sorted out the stack of typing which lay at the side of the computer.

At twelve o'clock he emerged from his office and informed her that he would be out for the rest of the day. She watched as he slipped on his jacket, adjusted his tie, and breathed a sigh of relief when the door closed behind him.

He made her tense and it wasn't simply due to the insults which he had flung at her. There was something watchful about him—something that stirred a certain uneasy wariness in her. He was like a shark, circling the water around her, content to watch, but she would do well to remember that sharks bit.

He had left her enough work to fill her time until five o'clock, but in fact she stayed on until nearly six-thirty, familiarising herself with his filing system, and familiarising herself also with some of the books on the shelf which he had informed her would have to be read, digested and memorised.

She had no idea how much of that had been said because he contemptuously believed that she would never manage such a task, but if she was to stay working with the loathsome man then she would make damned sure that by the end of her stint he would have to swallow everything he had said.

Her father was not at home when she got back—tired, but oddly elated at having spent the day doing something productive—but Rupert was. Bridie had let him in and Francesca found him in the sitting room, on his second glass of gin and tonic.

He looked at her as she walked in and said without preamble, 'Nasty rumour has it that you've got a job.'

Francesca looked at him and grinned. She was very fond of Rupert Thompson. She had known him casually for two years, but it was really only in the last seven months that they had become close, much to her father's disgust. He had no patience with men like Rupert. He thought that he should buckle down and find himself a job or, failing that, join the Army—as if joining the Army would suddenly change sunny-tempered Rupert into an aggressive work-machine.

The only thing that held him in check was his daughter's repeated reassurance that nothing was going on between them. Rupert was fun. He didn't want her as a passionate lover and the feeling was mutual.

She took off her coat, tossed it onto a chair and went across to the bar to pour herself a glass of mineral water.

'Nasty rumour,' she said, sitting down on the sofa, kicking off her shoes and tucking her feet underneath her, 'is right.' She looked at him. 'You could always follow my example,' she added, and he grinned at her infectiously.

'And lose my reputation? Never.'

As it happened, he did have a job of sorts, but in typical Rupert-style he had long ago decided that delegation was a talent that was much underrated. And, in fairness, it worked for him. His parents had died ten years ago, leaving him a fortune, along with a vast estate which he had happily left in the efficient hands of the managers who had looked after it from the year dot.

He signed things that needed his signature, spent enough time at his country home to ensure that things were being run profitably, and there his input ceased. He made sure that all his employees were treated well, received unstinting loyalty in return, and cheerfully had his good times on some of the immense profits that came his way.

'So tell all,'' he commanded, settling back comfortably with his drink, and Francesca obliged, carefully editing out the unpleasantness of her interview. She wasn't given to confiding private feelings to other people—a legacy, she had always assumed, of having been the only child of a single-parent family.

'Kemp,' Rupert murmured thoughtfully. 'Kemp, Kemp, Kemp. I know that name.'

'Their electronic stuff is all over the country, Rupert,' Francesca said drily. 'And they're branching out all the time,' she heard herself saying. 'They've moved into Europe and are hoping to capture the Far East fairly soon.' One *day*, she thought suddenly, and I sound like an advertising brochure. Had Oliver Kemp been that successful in influencing her thoughts? She found the idea of that slightly disconcerting.

'No, no, no.' He waved aside the explanation. 'What I mean is this—I've heard of that man personally.'

'Really?' She felt a sudden rush of curiosity which, she told herself, she had no intention of satisfying. Oliver Kemp was an arrogant bastard, and whatever he did in his private life had nothing to do with her. She would work for him because a combination of pride and guilt would make her, at least for the time being, but beyond that her interest stopped.

Rupert, immune to subtle shifts in atmosphere, blithely ignored this one and continued in the same thoughtful voice, 'Oliver Kemp. I've seen him around.'

'You've seen most people around,' she pointed out. 'You're hardly one of life's shrinking violets, are you?'

He laughed, pleased at that. 'Good-looking chap,' he said, draining his drink and eyeing the empty glass meaningfully. She ignored the hint. As far as she was concerned he drank too much anyway, and she had no intention of assisting the situation.

'You can have some mineral water, Rupert,' she said eventually, and he sighed in resignation.

'Too much of this stuff is bad for you,' he said when she handed him the glass of water. 'Haven't you heard that?'

'No, and nor have you.'

'A glass of wine, according to the experts, does wonders for some organ or other. Heart, I believe.'

'I would sympathise if your input was restricted to one glass per day.'

'Oliver Kemp,' he said, not commenting on that one, 'was in the gossip columns not too long ago. That's why the name rings a bell. Don't you ever read the gossip columns?'

'Too trivial,' she replied airily, and he laughed with great humour.

'Ever since they announced that we were about to become engaged?'

'Stupid people.' Her mouth tightened as she remembered all the fuss. One casual shot of them leaving a nightclub in London had been enough to propel them into an item, and it had been that silly drama which had led to all her father's unfounded suspicions that his daughter was about to do something utterly ridiculous.

'Well, they had their facts right about Oliver Kemp. He's engaged to a woman—Imogen something or other. There was a picture of them taken at their engagement party not too long ago.'

'Oliver Kemp is engaged?' Her voice was high and incredulous, and Rupert looked at her with some surprise.

'Sattler,' he said, nodding, delighted at this triumph of memory. 'Imogen Sattler. She's one of the city's top businesswomen. They squeezed in a few lines of background on her. Born up north somewhere.' He frowned. Instant recall was not one of his strong points and he didn't pursue it. 'Girl makes good, type of thing. You know what I mean—parents not well off, daughter very clever, gets into Oxford University, ends up sitting on the board of one of the top companies in the country.'

That made sense. Oliver thought that she was frivolous, an intellectual lightweight who spent her time enjoying her father's wealth—'Daddy's money' would probably be the term he would use, she thought with sudden bitterness. She was a decorative little bauble who had suddenly found herself catapulted into his sphere.

Rupert was standing up, ready to leave. He had only

really dropped by, he told her, to ask her out to dinner. 'Now that you're earning,' he said, 'I shall expect you to pay your way.'

'Rupert, I always pay my way, and let's not go into those times when your wallet has mysteriously been absent without leave.'

They laughed, and arranged a place to meet tomorrow—at seven, so that she would have time to leave work at six, dash back to the house, and quickly change.

She knew that she didn't need to justify herself in the eyes of Oliver Kemp, but some part of her wanted to prove to him that she wasn't the brainless dimwit he thought she was.

He had expected her to falter over that typing test, she realised, and he probably confidently expected that she wouldn't last the course in the job. He would think that she would get bored or that she wouldn't be able to cope, or both.

She went upstairs to have a bath, and by the time she emerged she had gone from simmering irritation over his contempt for her to downright anger. She had also found herself giving far too much thought to this fiancée of his.

She had no idea what Imogen Sattler looked like, but her imagination provided her with all the details—tall, hard, eyes as condescending and intolerant as his—the sort of woman who was only happy when discussing the stock market or the economy, the sort of woman who never *spoke* but *held forth* to an audience. The sort of woman, in fact, who would be ideally suited to a man like Oliver Kemp. And, of course, they would share the same hard edge of people born without comforts and destined to make their own.

Her father came home just as Francesca was finishing her meal and settling down to a cup of coffee. It took a great deal of effort to maintain a calm expression, to convince herself that working for Oliver Kemp was worth it when she saw how his face lit up at the thought that his dear little daughter had taken the bull by the horns and got herself a job—and one that he had recommended at that.

And he must have known Oliver Kemp's character more than he had originally suggested, because he was visibly relieved when she told him that the job was fine, that the boss was fine, that everything would work out, she was sure. She kept her fingers crossed behind her back all the while.

'He's a very highly respected man,' her father said, prepared to be just the tiniest bit smug.

Francesca made agreeing noises and thought, Respected by whom? Vampires and other creatures of the night?

But then, she later thought in bed, he wasn't coldhearted, was he? Not with a fiancée tucked away in the background.

She tried to imagine him as a hot-blooded man of passion, and that was so easy that by the time she finally fell asleep she no longer felt just angry and resentful towards him, she also felt vaguely disturbed.

CHAPTER TWO

'So you made it here on time.'

Those were the first words that greeted Francesca as she walked through the office door at five minutes to nine. She had planned on arriving earlier, but her body had become accustomed to late mornings, and trying to put it through its paces at seven-thirty had been torturous.

She looked at him, keeping her temper in check, but he wasn't looking at her at all.

'I see you managed to finish all the typing that was on your desk. What time did you leave last night?'

Francesca sat down at her desk. She had dressed in slightly more conservative clothes today—navy blue dress, straight and fairly shapeless and far less obviously designer.

'Around six,' she murmured vaguely, and his eyes slid across to her with irony.

'There's no need to become a workhorse,' he said mildly, reaching down two volumes from the shelf of books and putting them on the desk next to her. 'I want hard work out of you; I don't want a nervous breakdown.'

'What is that supposed to mean?' she asked, eyeing the books.

'What it's supposed to mean is that I don't want you working over-long hours and then complaining of exhaustion by the end of the week.'

'I'm not a complaining sort, Mr Kemp,' she answered, truthfully enough, and he shrugged, not really interested in what she was or wasn't, she supposed, just so long as it didn't intrude on work.

It was a novel situation. She had always been accustomed to provoking a reaction in men. She had the extraordinary looks of a blonde with contrasting dark eyes and eyebrows. She looked at him from under her thick lashes and saw that as far as her looks were concerned she might well be as alluring to him as the umbrella stand in the corner of the office.

'I want you to get a start on these two books,' he said, pushing his hands into his pockets. 'They'll give you some background information on what the company does. Before that you'd better come into my office and we'll go through my work diary for the next six months.'

She followed him into the office and obediently compared her thick diary with his, slotting in meetings and conferences which had obviously been arranged since the departure of his last unsuccessful temp.

When he had finished he sat back in his chair and looked at her steadily.

What was it, she wondered, about this man's eyes? They were quite cool, quite calculating, but somewhere in the wintry depths there was also something else—something offputtingly sexual.

'I never got around to asking you whether you have any questions about the company,' he said, 'or, for that matter, about your role in it. Have you?'

'What did your last secretary do?' Francesca asked 'I mean, the one who left three years ago. What duties did she have?'

He looked at her with a trace of irony on his mouth. 'Do you intend to fill her shoes?' he asked. 'No one else has managed that.'

'I'm willing to give it a try,' she said evenly. 'I know you don't think very much of me—'

'Oh, but I think your secretarial skills are surprisingly as good as your father described.' His voice was cool and his choice of words blunt enough to leave her in no doubt as to where the remainder of his thoughts lay.

Francesca kept her temper. She was normally an even-tempered person, but then, admittedly, no one had ever been quite so abrupt to her before. She had only been in the job one day but already she was beginning to realise exactly how cushioned her life had been. When she walked into the building she was surrounded by people purpose-fully going somewhere, hurrying to jobs because, no doubt, they needed the pay-packet that came with employment.

'Irene,' he said into the silence, 'was my right-hand man. She not only typed, she also knew the workings of this company almost as well as I do. When I asked for information on a client she could provide it almost without needing to go to a file for reference.'

'Sounds a paragon,' Francesca said wryly.

'I think it's called devotion. The assortment of sec-retaries I've had since then have been in the job simply for the money.'

'Which,' she pointed out, 'is one thing, at least, you can't accuse me of.'

'No,' he returned without emphasis, 'but your lack of need to earn a living does mean that it's fairly immaterial what you bring to this job, wouldn't you agree?'

'You're not prepared to give me a fighting chance, are you?' she asked, and he shrugged, neither confirming or denying that. He simply continued to look at her steadily, shrewdly, with cool judgement in his pale eyes.

'How did you start all this?' she asked, changing the

subject because she didn't want to let him get under her skin. Again.

'With a loan from the bank,' he replied drily, as if it had been a particularly stupid question because the answer was so self-evident.

'And after the loan from the bank came what?'

'A small outlet in the Midlands. Our products were good, though, and we moved in at a fortuitous point in the market. Any more questions?'

He waited politely and she clamped her teeth together. It wasn't difficult to tell that he found her a bore. She stood up, shaking her head, and when she looked back towards him as she left his office his attention was already elsewhere, his face frowning as he skimmed through something on the computer on his desk.

She quietly closed the door behind her, feeling for almost the first time in her life that she had been politely rebuffed.

When you thought about it, she decided, it was funny— funny to have the shoe on the other foot, not to be the focus of admiring attention. Except that she didn't much feel like laughing, even though she knew that her reactions were childish and that she would have to stop acting like a damned spoiled brat who sulked when she was not in the limelight. She had never before considered herself a spoiled brat and it was silly acting like one, she told herself, just because Oliver Kemp, a man whom she didn't like anyway, found her uninteresting.

At ten-thirty the outer door opened and one of the managers strolled in. He was in his mid-thirties, fair-haired, and the minute he saw her his eyebrows flew up.

'Well,' he drawled, darting a quick eye at the connecting door and then obviously deciding that the coast was clear, 'where have you been hiding yourself, my lovely?'

Francesca stopped what she was doing and said calmly, 'You must be Mr Robinson. Mr Kemp is expecting you. I'll just buzz and tell him that you've arrived.'

'Brad. And no need just yet. I'm five minutes early anyway.' He eyed the door again and adjusted his flamboyantly coloured tie.

Francesca watched him in silence as he perched familiarly on the edge of her desk and leant towards her. She knew this type, this make and model.

'When did the wind blow you in?' he asked.

Probably married, she thought, but still felt as though he was entitled by divine right to do just whatsoever he pleased. Probably, she decided, he felt as though it was his duty to spread himself around the female population, or at least around those remotely presentable.

'I've been here since yesterday,' Francesca answered coolly, 'and I wasn't blown in by the wind.'

'No, but you look as though you should have been. Ethereal, almost, with that hair of yours.' He reached out to touch her hair, and she saw Oliver Kemp watching them with widening eyes. How long had he been standing there? She hadn't heard the click of his door opening.

'Mr Kemp,' she said, standing up, 'I was just about to show Mr Robinson in.'

Mr Robinson had gone an embarrassed shade of red and had hopped off the desk as though suddenly discovering that it was made of burning embers.

Oliver didn't say a word, and his dark-fringed, pale eyes were expressionless. He simply turned his back. The now very subdued manager bustled in behind him and the door was firmly shut.

Francesca released a long breath. She felt inappropriately as though she had been caught red-handed doing something unthinkable.

When an hour and a half later Brad Robinson hurried out of the office, making sure not to look in her direction, she found that she was concentrating a little too hard on what she was doing, and when Oliver Kemp moved across to her desk the colour flooded into her face.

'I do apologise,' she began, stammering, and he looked at her with raised eyebrows.

'By all means. What for, though?'

She had been so sure that he had been going to say something to her, in that coldly sarcastic way of his, about not flirting with management that his question took her by surprise.

'I didn't invite Mr Robinson to sit on my desk...' she began, faltering and going a deeper red. 'He—'

'He's an inveterate flirt, Miss Wade,' Oliver cut in unsmilingly. 'I've caught him sitting on more desktops than I care to remember, but he's a damned good salesman.'

'Of course,' she murmured with relief.

'That's not to say that I condone a lot of time-wasting during office hours,' he added.

'No.' She paused. 'Though I know how to handle men like Brad Robinson, anyway.'

'I'm sure. I expect you're quite accustomed to men who flirt the minute they clap eyes on you.'

He didn't say that as a compliment and he was already looking at his watch.

'I've got a few files here,' he said, moving round the desk and perching next to her. Her eyes travelled along his muscular forearms to where his sleeves were rolled up to the elbows, and she felt a sudden twinge of uneasy awareness.

'Yes, sir,' she mumbled, disconcerted by her reaction.

His dark-fringed eyes slid across to hers and he said drily, 'You can call me Oliver. I don't believe in a hierarchical system, where my employees salute every time I walk past. Bad for the morale.'

'You've studied psychology?' Francesca asked, and he raised his eyebrows. 'I'm sorry,' she said, flustered, 'I...'

'Don't mean to be sarcastic all the time?' He sat on the edge of the desk. 'I suspect that that's because you've never had to curb your tongue, have you?'

'What do you mean?'

'What I mean, Miss Wade, is that your privileged background has opened a great many doors for you. People are often subservient to wealth, and I suspect that you've come to expect subservience as part and parcel of everyday life.'

'That's not true,' she said in a weak voice, but there was more than an ounce of truth in what he was saying. She had not gone through life demanding special treatment, but on the other hand it had frequently been given to her.

'This is your first job,' he continued relentlessly, 'and probably for the first time in your life you're going to have to realise that no one here is going to treat you as anything other than another employee in this organisation.' She felt his cold blue eyes skewering into her dispassionately.

'I don't want to be treated any differently from anyone else,' Francesca said defensively. She looked away from the hard, sexy contours of his face, which anyway was only addling her mind still further, and stared at the stack of files on which his hand was resting.

'I'm glad to hear it.' He slipped off the desk and turned his attention back to the files. 'There are letters in these which need typing and I've highlighted a few things which I want you to sort out. You'll have to phone the regional managers and arrange appointments for them to come and see me. As far as the Smith Holdings one is concerned, make sure that you get Jeffrey Lake to see me no later than lunchtime tomorrow.' He looked down at her. 'Any questions?'

'I don't think so,' Francesca murmured, and a ghost of a smile crossed his face.

'You're very confident, aren't you?'

'Don't tell me that there's something wrong with that!'

'Nothing at all.'

She looked up at him and their eyes met. 'I guess you'd be able to analyse that trait in me as well? Wealth breeds self-confidence, doesn't it? Maybe you start off from the vantage point of thinking that everyone is inferior, so it's an easy step towards thinking that you're capable of anything.'

'Very good,' he drawled, and his expression was veiled. 'Too much self-confidence is as bad as too little, though. I'm sure you wouldn't like to fall flat on your face just because you're too proud to ask questions.'

'I don't intend to fall flat on my face,' she returned calmly, 'and I'm not so completely stupid that I don't realise the value of asking questions when I need to.'

'Good.' He walked towards the door and she watched his loose-limbed stride with angry fascination. 'I won't be back for the rest of the day,' he said over his shoulder. 'If you need me I'll be contactable on my mobile phone until seven, then anything after that will have to wait until tomorrow.'

Once he had gone she turned to the computer and methodically began working her way through the files, calling the regional managers, arranging appointments.

Every so often, though, her mind would flit back to him. It irked her that he treated her like a child—an over-indulged child who appeared capable of handling the job but of not much else beyond that. There was always a cool dismissiveness in his voice when he addressed her, and even when he had perched on the desk and offered her his little pearls of insight into her personality the basic uninterest had still been there. To him she was a case study in everything that he disapproved of. Someone who would either do her job well or not.

Her father, had he known, would have had a good laugh at that, she thought.

She worked steadily through lunch, and it was only when the door was pushed open that she realised with some surprise that it was after four.

'Hi.'

One word—a monosyllable—and Francesca knew instantly that she wasn't going to warm to the girl standing by her desk, looking at her with assessing eyes.

'What can I do for you?'

'Could you give these to your boss for signing? I take it he's not in.'

'No. Who shall I say left them?'

'Helen. I work in the accounts department.'

She looked, Francesca thought, as though she had been wildly miscast. She looked, in fact, as though she should have been working at the cosmetic counter of a large department store. Her hair, dyed jet-black, was carefully styled and hung in a straight bob to her shoulders, and her face was impeccably made up in an assortment of shades which gave her the look of a highly painted doll—she was attractive in a very obvious sort of way, and was clearly in no mood to hurry on, from the way she was standing looking around her.

'Actually,' Helen said, dragging a chair to sit opposite Francesca, much to Francesca's dismay, 'we've been curious about you. One minute Oliver had given his temp the boot and Cathy was filling in, and the next minute here you are. How did you manage to land the job?'

'Oh, usual way,' Francesca lied vaguely, but the other girl let that one go past. She was clearly not madly interested in the ins and outs of how Francesca had found herself working for Oliver Kemp. But she wanted something, because she still made no move to depart.

'We're all dying of envy, anyway,' Helen said, narrowing her blue eyes. 'I'd do anything to work for Oliver, but my typing skills are lousy.' She picked up a paperweight from the desk and idly turned it over while Francesca wondered what this bizarre conversation was leading to.

'Well, I'm sure your job must be very interesting,' Francesca said politely, and Helen laughed—a hard, brittle sound that jarred.

'Oh, riveting, dear.' She plonked the paperweight back down and stood up. 'Well, I'm off; just thought I'd come and see what the competition was like.'

'The competition?'

'Oh, yes.' She opened her eyes wide and failed to look guileless. 'Thought you might be the brainy type that Oliver goes for, but you're not. Still, just between the two of us, he can't be that immune to a pretty face, can he?'

'And, if he isn't, you want to make sure that you're the one in the firing-line?'

'Got it in one.' She smiled but without humour. 'I'd give my right arm to get into the sack with him.'

'Really?'

'Wouldn't you?'

'No,' Francesca said coldly. 'Now, if you don't mind, I've got a lot of work to do.'

'Sure.' Helen walked towards the door. 'He in tomorrow?' she asked, and Francesca nodded. 'Tell him I'll come by to collect that stuff in the morning.' And she was gone, leaving an unpleasant taste in Francesca's mouth.

That, she thought acidly, was office politics—something else of which she had no experience.

She was ready to leave by five-thirty, and it was something of a relief to see Rupert at seven—sweet, uncomplicated Rupert, who wouldn't know the meaning of 'connive' if it jumped in front of him waving a sign in neon lettering.

'You look tired,' he said as they walked towards his car—a sleek red Jaguar which he had obligingly parked in the very centre of the courtyard. 'Tired yet extraordinarily gorgeous, considering all we're doing is going out for a meal. Sure you won't change your mind about coming out to a nightclub with me? We could dance till dawn and drink until at least midnight.'

Francesca laughed. He was incorrigible. He was also easy company. They drove to the restaurant—a French bistro in the theatre district—and he entertained her with a barrage of fairly trivial chat, which was quite amusing nevertheless. Rupert had always felt uncomfortable with pregnant pauses in conversation, and consequently he was adept at making small talk, which, she thought as they went into the restaurant, was just what she needed.

The restaurant was dimly lit, in accordance with someone's clever notion that subdued lighting was conducive to a romantic atmosphere.

The proprietor knew them well and showed them to a little table in the corner, much loved by aficionados because it offered an excellent view of the other diners. Rupert liked it. From there he could watch the comings and goings of the largely pre and post theatre crowd who were wealthy enough to afford the exorbitant prices the place charged.

Privileges, Francesca thought suddenly—all those privileges that money could buy.

She had never known what it was like to have her choice of restaurant narrowed down to a hamburger bar because of financial considerations. Of course, she had eaten hamburgers, and she had enjoyed them, but then she had chosen to. She frowned and wondered why she was devoting so much time to these questions when they had never really bothered her before.

She was subdued over the meal, listening to Rupert ramble on in his harmless, amusing fashion. He was typical of all her friends—out for a good time, ever game for harmless, mostly expensive fun. But they all lacked something, didn't they? she thought. It was as though reality hadn't quite impinged upon them.

Then she thought of Oliver Kemp, and that irritated her. He was hardly what she would call a role model of a caring man—at least not as far as he had shown her—but still, he was somehow more substantial than anyone else she had ever met, wasn't he?

Rupert was saying something and she nodded amiably enough, letting her eyes drift through the crowded restaurant, and she saw him just as he saw her. Their eyes tangled in the dimly lit room, and then, with a feeling of sinking horror, she watched as he and his companion walked towards their table.

At first she hardly noticed the woman with him. The only thing her eyes could focus on was the masculine figure in his dark suit with a cream silk tie around his neck.

'Oh, God, Rupert,' she whispered nervously. 'Here comes my boss.'

They watched until Oliver had approached the table, then Rupert, ever ready with a tactless opening statement, said, smiling broadly, 'So you're the slave-driver I've been hearing so much about!' He stood up, unruffled by Oliver's cool, speculative expression, and said expansively, 'Why don't you pull up a couple of pews and join us?'

'I'm sure Mr Kemp has a table booked,' Francesca said, mortified, while the woman with him watched the cabaret with a pleasant smile.

'We'd love to join you,' she said, still smiling, and for the first time Francesca looked at her fully.

Was this Imogen Sattler—the tall, hard woman she had envisaged from Rupert's vague description? The self-made woman who had climbed to the top of her career?

She was small, with short, curly fair hair and an intelligently serious face.

'I take it you've just come from a play?' Rupert asked them both as they sat down, and Oliver nodded, looking at Francesca with amusement, as though the playboy man in her life was just precisely as he had imagined.

'I'm Rupert Thompson, by the way,' Rupert said with limitless *bonhomie*. 'General wastrel but with a heart of gold.'

The woman laughed and said brightly, 'What a novel introduction. I'm Imogen Sattler.' She looked at Francesca. 'And I'm so glad to meet you. I hope you work out as Oliver's secretary. He seems to run through them at a rate of knots.' She glanced at him fondly, and Francesca felt a spurt of confused emotion which she could neither explain nor rationalise.

'So I understand,' she said politely, looking at Oliver from under her lashes.

'Miss Wade is still in the enthusiastic phase,' Oliver said coolly. 'She's trying to prove herself.'

That amused Rupert. He beamed, took a generous sip of port, and said, grinning, 'That must be new to her.

You've never had to prove yourself to anyone before, have you, Frankie?'

If he had set out to confirm everything that Oliver suspected of her, he couldn't have done it better. Oliver gave her a dry, knowing look, and she said defensively, 'Of course I'm not trying to prove myself. I just feel that if I'm employed to do a job of work then I should do it thoroughly.'

'Well done!' Imogen said, laughing. 'Just don't let him take advantage of you! He's notorious for taking advantage of his secretaries. Why do you think they all leave with such alarming regularity?'

'Now, now,' Oliver murmured, and his light eyes slid across to his fiancée, 'you make me sound like an ogre.'

The waiter approached to take their order and Rupert said, speaking for all of them, 'Just the bill. Our friends here have decided to come to a nightclub with us. Haven't you?' He looked at Imogen and murmured breezily, 'It would be a shame to waste such a glamorous outfit on a badly lit restaurant, don't you agree?'

She looked delighted at this turn in events, but Oliver's mouth had thinned and he said abruptly, 'I don't think so.'

'I'd really like to just get home, Rupert,' Francesca said, alarmed, but he waved aside both protests as if the thought of their turning down his kind invitation was hardly conceivable.

'Nonsense, Frankie. Just because you've got a job it doesn't mean that you have to give up all of life's little pleasures.'

'It would be fun,' Imogen said, turning to Oliver, and he looked at her with grudging indulgence.

They might not be all over each other, Francesca thought, but there was a thread of real emotion there between them, evident in the way they looked at one another.

Was this love? She abruptly drained her glass of port and felt a little dizzy.

Rupert stood up and held his arm out for Imogen. 'You don't mind my escorting your lovely fiancée to the door, do you, old man?'

Oliver was beginning to look mildly irritated, and when he fell into step with Francesca he said in a low, harsh voice, 'Can't you keep a rein on your lover?'

'Rupert is not my lover!' she said angrily, and he shrugged.

'Whatever, then. Playmate.'

'You make us sound like a couple of children.'

They were walking towards the door, and ahead of them Imogen was laughing, highly entertained by whatever Rupert was saying. He could be a superb conversationalist when he chose—witty, warm, direct, and with a boyish charm that could halt a charging rhino at a hundred paces. Francesca had seen it in action often enough before.

'And it's hardly my fault that Rupert's commandeered your fiancée, is it?' she added tartly.

'Oh, Imogen is a big girl,' Oliver drawled lazily. 'And intelligent enough not to be taken in by your little playmate's oily charm.'

They stepped outside into the freezing air, and Rupert immediately hailed a taxi while Imogen smiled coaxingly at Oliver over her shoulder. 'We never go to nightclubs,' she said persuasively, her eyes bright. 'It might be fun!'

Francesca thought that going to sleep sounded rather more fun, and her mouth was tight by the time the taxi pulled up to the nightclub and deposited them outside.

Rupert was well-known there, not that it would have mattered. Oliver's presence commanded such immediate awe that they were ushered in like royalty, and Francesca looked around at the familiar haunt with a sinking heart.

Had she really enjoyed frequenting these places—loud music, beautiful people frenetically talking and looking around them, eyes ever open to spot anyone they knew?

'I'm awfully sorry about this,' she murmured to Imogen once they were inside, and the other woman turned to her with wry humour in her eyes.

'Why? It makes a change for me. My head is normally so full of business that I find it hard to relax.'

Oliver, with an ease which he seemed to accept without question as people made way for him, had gone to the bar for drinks, and Imogen took her arm confidentially.

'You come here often, I gather?'

'Oh, all the time,' Francesca said, airily. 'My head is so devoid of business that I find it terribly easy to relax.'

'I wasn't meaning to be offensive,' Imogen said with gentle sincerity, and Francesca blushed.

'No, of course not; it's just...'

'That Oliver's been giving you a hard time because of your background? He told me that your father is terribly well off.'

'And what else has he told you?' She pictured them together, talking about her, and winced.

'He's a hard man,' Imogen said, 'but I expect you'll get used to that in time. If you stick it out, that is! Must be something of a culture shock, though,' she added thoughtfully, 'if you're used to a man like Rupert.'

'Rupert,' Francesca began defensively, 'is—'

'A type of person I've never met in my life before!' Imogen laughed, and Francesca felt the beginnings of real warmth towards her. She watched as Rupert took her to the dance floor and reluctantly sat down in a secluded corner with Oliver.

Out of the corner of her eye she could see the attention he was receiving from other women in the room—sidelong glances of interest which he either chose to ignore or else genuinely didn't notice.

'I can understand why your father was worried about your lifestyle,' he said, leaning towards her.

Amidst the noise and push of people there was something disturbingly intimate about his husky voice, and she looked at him and felt a twinge of something uninvited begin to stir inside her. She pushed it aside and said crisply, 'I never intended to make this kind of thing a permanent feature of my life.'

'You just spent the past few months allowing yourself to be persuaded into it?'

'That's hardly fair! You don't know me.'

'I know enough.' He looked around him and there was a condescending glitter in his pale eyes which made the blood rush to her head angrily.

'Your fiancée seems to be enjoying it,' she snapped.

'The element of novelty has its temptations for a limited period of time.'

'You sound as though you've never had a moment's fun in your life before.'

'Is that what you think?' He refocused his attention on her, and she felt her head begin to swim a little.

'Well, have you?'

'I didn't spend my whole life in front of books before joining the army of people out to earn a living,' he replied, his deep, low voice cutting through the tinny sound of the music.

'You just decided somewhere along the line that fun was something you could do without?' She cradled her glass in her hands, unwilling to drink another drop because she already felt a bit giddy.

'No, I just decided that this sort of thing was an exercise in stupidity.'

'Which I suppose is another criticism of me?'

He shrugged. 'You can suppose anything you like.'

'You don't really care one way or the other.' For some reason that stung.

'That's right.' He leaned back in his chair and looked at his watch.

'I'll make sure that I'm at work on time tomorrow,' Francesca said, abandoning her principles and taking another long gulp of her drink.

'Of course you will,' he murmured easily, 'if only to prove that you can burn the candle at both ends and still function.'

'I don't have to prove anything to you,' Francesca lied, not meeting his eyes.

'Well, then,' he said, not bothering to look at her, 'maybe to yourself.'

CHAPTER THREE

'I'M LEAVING home.' Francesca's father looked at her with anxious consternation, and she knew that it wasn't because of what she had just announced but the way she had announced it. She knew that her mouth was tight, her words abrupt, her expression hard, but she was just so angry that anything else was quite beyond her.

How could he?

'I've found a flat,' she carried on, not quite meeting her father's eyes but not looking away either. 'It's small but it'll do, and I shall move at the weekend. You're away for a couple of weeks so I won't get under your feet.'

'What's the matter?'

'What's the matter?' She stood up and walked across the room to the window, then she turned to face him, her hands on her hips. 'Dad, how *could* you?'

Two months, she thought furiously; two months of working for Oliver Kemp and now this. She didn't quite know how the sudden flare-up had happened. She had got into work the morning before and had known the minute she had clapped eyes on him that he was in a foul temper.

Whether it had been his mood or a reaction to two months of his stunning indifference to her, which, she had managed to persuade herself, suited her just fine, she didn't quite know, but she had snapped.

All she could coherently remember was Oliver leaning across her desk with a filthy expression on his face and telling her that the document which she had typed, which she had spent *hours* typing, would have to be redone because some of the facts were inaccurate, and that she should have known better. As if, she had thought at the time, she were on some uncanny hotline to Divine Company Information.

David Bass had dictated the facts. How could she have known that some of them weren't on target? She had said as much to Oliver.

'Oh, I've had a few words with David Bass,' Oliver had said grimly, and then she had snapped.

'How could I *what*?' her father asked now, and she glared at him. The memory of what Oliver had told her was still humiliatingly clear in her head.

'How could you have blackmailed Oliver Kemp into hiring me?' she wailed, angry with her father, herself, Oliver and the world at large.

She had spent the last two months working hard, proving herself, foolishly believing that she had got the job on her own merit, and she knew that she would have continued harbouring the illusion if she hadn't goaded Oliver into revealing the truth.

Her father was looking uncomfortable, clearing his throat and attempting to placate her, but Francesca was in no mood to forgive.

'I only did it for your own good, my dear,' he offered.

'You knew his father very well, didn't you, Dad?' she said bitterly. 'This was no passing acquaintance you bumped into accidentally. You grew up with his father! You both went to the same school, except that when you left to go on to a private school to finish your education he left to support a family of nine!'

'He was a very clever man,' her father murmured ruefully, which to her seemed quite beside the point.

'I don't care if he was Einstein!' Francesca shouted, on the point of tears. 'Oliver said that when his father died you sent them money—money so that Oliver could have the education he deserved. You sent me to him like a mouse to a trap, knowing that he would have no option but to employ me.'

'You went of your own free will,' her father pointed out, and Francesca ignored him.

'You put him in a position of obligation. I was a debt.' Her voice sank to a whisper. 'A debt to be paid off.'

'I knew you could do the job,' her father said.

'In that case you should have let me prove myself,' she retorted immediately, and her father reddened.

'My dear—' he began, and she cut him short with a wave of her hand.

'No,' she said, gathering herself together. 'It's done, but I shall never forgive you for this.'

'You're making a mountain out of a molehill. If Oliver had thought you incompetent he would have sacked you, debt or no debt.'

'The fact is you shouldn't have blackmailed him.' She walked towards the door. 'Please tell Bridie that I'll be in over the weekend to get my things together.' She didn't want to meet her father's eye. Her anger was so great that it pushed aside everything else. It consumed her.

'I can't possibly continue working for you,' she had told Oliver the day before, shaken and humiliated by his revelation.

And he had said curtly, 'Don't be a complete fool. I won't accept a resignation from you.'

'Why?' she had taunted bitterly. 'Because you're hon-our-bound to keep me here?'

'And stop,' he had said, unwittingly focusing on the one thing guaranteed to make her feel even worse, 'acting like a child.'

She felt like a child now, but she couldn't help herself.

Her self-respect had been whipped away and she felt naked and vulnerable, and she certainly wasn't about to be persuaded by her father to be reasonable.

She didn't want to be reasonable. She wanted to fling things about, and before she could do that she left, slamming the door behind her and bringing Bridie rushing down the stairs to see what was wrong.

Francesca was still fuming the following morning when she got to work, and as soon as Oliver walked in and saw her face he said tightly, impatiently, 'For God's sake, Francesca, drop it.'

'Drop what?' She watched as he took off his jacket, then slowly turned around to face her.

'Let's get one thing straight,' he said, moving across to her desk and propping himself on it with his hands. 'If I hadn't thought that you could do the job I wouldn't have hired you.'

'Sure,' Francesca muttered under her breath, and he gripped her chin with his fingers, forcing her to look at him.

'I can't stand people who feel sorry for themselves,' he grated, and she met his eyes with an angry glare.

'Since you can't stand me anyway,' she said, 'I don't think any further criticisms of my character will have any effect.'

He shook his head and looked as if he could willingly have slapped her, but instead he stood up and strode into his office, slamming the door behind him.

By the time Friday rolled around Francesca's nerves were jangling from the silently aggressive atmosphere between them.

Her work was as efficient as ever, but her body tensed

the minute he came near her, and there was a tension in him too that didn't help matters. She still hadn't told him that she was moving house, and she delayed that until she was ready to leave on the Friday evening, when she said coolly, not looking at him, 'I don't know whether I mentioned this to you or not, but I've decided to leave home.'

'Why?'

She shrugged and headed towards the door, but he was there before her, and he positioned himself right in front of it so that she had to stay where she was.

'I've decided that accepting charity from you is bad enough, but accepting it from my father as well is just compounding the situation.'

'And what exactly is the situation, Francesca?' he asked unsmilingly. 'That you've been knocked off course by something I shouldn't have said, and you're not big enough to believe me when I tell you that it doesn't really matter?'

'Yes, that's it,' she said flippantly. 'I'm not big enough.'

His lips thinned. 'Your father once did me a favour, and in return I did him one. Leave it at that.'

Francesca remained silent, her face quietly stubborn, and he shook his head with impatience.

'You're about to tell me that I'm acting like a child,' she said to him. 'Aren't you?'

'You read minds as well, do you?'

'Only yours,' she retorted, saying the first thing that sprang to her lips, and there was a thick silence in which an intimacy which had not been there before seemed to take shape and hover between them.

'Don't blame your father,' he said, looking away from her with a dull flush on his cheeks. 'He only did it for you.' He paused. 'I'll need your address for Personnel. They'll have to have their files updated. I'm on my way to see Sally now, so I'll tell her.' His voice sounded odd, but when he met her eyes again it was with his usual expression of inscrutability.

She rattled off the address, which she knew he had no need to write down because he stored things in his memory with prodigious ease.

'Take a couple of days off,' he said, stepping aside from the door so that she could leave.

She replied immediately, 'No, thank you.'

'No,' he murmured, 'I thought not.' Then he walked back into his office and shut the door behind him, and she cranked her mind away from him and onto the matter at hand—the move.

It didn't take long. By seven-thirty the following evening she had transferred everything she was taking with her from her father's house to the flat.

Now, for the first time, she sat down on the tiny two-seater sofa squashed beneath the bay window and looked around her. It would take some getting used to, that was for sure. If her father's house had been a sprawling mansion, this in comparison was a doll's house.

It had one minuscule kitchen with a fridge that could hold a carton of eggs and not much else, one small bedroom with a bathroom adjacent to it, and a living room with a rather tired-looking sofa, two chairs, and a Persian rug which she had brought from her own bedroom and which looked arrogantly glamorous on the floor in front of the fireplace.

The ceilings were high, though, because it was a Victorian house, and although the place had been chopped about to accommodate six little flats, nothing could detract from the graceful lines of the building. She sat back and smiled a slow smile of pleasure.

This, she thought, was the first taste of real freedom she

had ever had, and although an unfortunate combination of events had brought her here it still felt good.

Money, her father had once told her years back, was a trap. She had never given the observation much thought, but now she could see how true the statement had been.

If you let it, money would give you everything, but it would also form the bars of your gilded cage, and there you could remain for ever, unable to break free.

There was a sharp knock on the door and she jumped up in some surprise to answer it. It couldn't be Rupert. He had ruefully told her that he was going out on Saturday night, and she hadn't as yet told any of her other friends that she had moved. Most of them would think her completely deranged, and she had lost touch with quite a few, anyway, since she had started work and no longer had time to fritter away the days.

Oliver Kemp, however, was the last person she had expected to see. She pulled open the door, and as soon as she saw his tall dark shape in the hall she felt her heart begin to thud.

He watched the fleeting expressions on her face and lounged indolently against the doorframe. 'Are you going to invite me in?' he asked. 'Or would you rather we just stand here and look at one another?'

Francesca dutifully stepped aside and he brushed past her, his powerful frame dwarfing the small dimensions of the room.

'What are you doing here?' she asked, shutting the door behind her. She felt scruffy in her jeans and faded blue and white checked shirt and at a disadvantage.

'I thought I'd bring you a house-warming present,' he said, prowling around the small sitting room and, en route, placing two bottles of cold champagne on the table in front of the sofa.

'That was very thoughtful of you.' She didn't move and he finally turned around to face her.

'Your voice rings with sincerity,' he drawled. 'Mind if I sit down?'

He did anyway, tossing his coat and jacket onto one of the chairs and rolling up the sleeves of his shirt.

'When you told me that you were moving into your own place, I have to admit that this wasn't quite what I had expected.'

'Oh, really?' She picked up the bottles of champagne, and eyed him warily through her lashes. 'Did you think that I would have found myself somewhere larger and more luxurious?'

'The thought had crossed my mind,' he admitted.

'I may have been born into luxury,' she said, still not willing to forgive him even though she had simmered down a little. 'It doesn't mean I'm addicted to it.'

'*Touché*' He stood up and went across to the kitchen, and after a while he emerged holding two glasses of champagne.

'You really don't have to stay here...' she began, unconsciously making sure that their fingers didn't touch as she took the glass from him.

'Do you want me to leave?'

'N-no, of c-course not...' Francesca stammered, feeling thoroughly out of her depth.

'Have you got someone else calling round?'

'No.'

'I wanted to make sure that you were all right,' he said, his fingers lightly caressing the stem of the glass.

'Why shouldn't I be?' She sipped some of the champagne.

'Because you're like a nervous thoroughbred, overreacting to things, rearing up at imaginary obstacles.'

'Thanks so much for the vote of confidence,' she snapped, ready to argue if that was what he wanted, but he unexpectedly laughed.

Francesca took another mouthful of champagne. She had never been a great lover of champagne. As far as she was concerned it was a hugely overrated drink, but she had to admit that its bubbles went to her head faster than lightning.

He looked at her over the rim of his glass.

'Why are you here, anyway?' she asked in hurried confusion. 'Where's Imogen?'

'Imogen,' he said evenly, 'is out. With your boyfriend, as a matter of fact.'

Francesca's mouth half opened in surprise. 'Rupert?' she asked stupidly.

'Do you have more than one boyfriend?'

'What is she doing with Rupert?'

'They've gone to a nightclub.'

'They've gone to a nightclub?'

'You sound shocked. What sort of relationship do you have with this man if you don't know what he does when you're not around?'

She was still too amazed to find a suitable retort to that. 'So that's why you're here,' she said, nodding her head slowly, and feeling deflated. 'You don't care about my mental welfare. You've come to have it out with me just because your fiancée has been seeing Rupert behind your back.' Actually, after a couple of glasses of champagne on an empty stomach, *she* was beginning to lose interest in her mental welfare as well.

His dark eyebrows flew up and he laughed. 'Have it out with you? Don't be puerile. Imogen tried to drag me along to the damned place but I decided I could do without the dubious pleasure of loud music and the inevitable headache.'

'But don't you mind?' Francesca asked, proffering her glass for some more champagne, and wondering how she had ever got so worked up over Oliver's revelation to her a few days before.

'Don't I mind what?'

'That your fiancée is out on the town with another man?'

'I'm not a jealous man, and besides—I think I told you this before—I trust Imogen. She's also a free being. I don't believe in putting someone under lock and key and claiming possession of them.'

'How very liberal-minded.'

She had hardly had anything alcoholic to drink for weeks, and her three glasses of champagne had gone to her head with alarming speed.

She tucked her feet back under her and heard herself saying, with the sudden insight of someone who has had one glass too many, 'Did you think that I might need bolstering at the thought of Rupert on the town with another woman?' She laughed, throwing her head back so that her hair spilled over the back of the chair in white-blonde disarray. 'Hardly! Rupert and I aren't lovers!'

His eyes narrowed on her, but he didn't comment. He said conversationally, 'How did your father react to your moving out?'

'He didn't try to stop me,' Francesca answered, circling the rim of her glass with one finger, then taking another sip from it.

'Would he have succeeded if he'd tried?'

'No.'

'Then he's a wise man.'

'When I told you that I wanted to leave I meant it,'

Francesca murmured, with a logic that only made sense to herself.

'Of course you didn't mean it.' She didn't look up but she could feel those amazing eyes on her. 'You like working for me, whether you want to admit it or not.'

'And do you like *me* working for *you*?' Francesca asked, topping up her glass with the remainder of the champagne from the bottle. 'You don't approve of me; you could have got rid of me for any number of reasons once you felt your debt had been paid in full.'

'I may not approve of you,' he said lazily, 'but I would have to dislike you personally to want that.'

Why didn't that make her feel any better? she wondered. Because, a hazy little voice murmured, you don't want to occupy that limbo between like and dislike, you want to be actively liked; in fact you want to be actively desired.

She felt her skin burn at the illogicality of that.

'Shall I open the other bottle of champagne?' she asked, not pursuing the unwelcome thought. She didn't wait for an answer. She went into the kitchen, opened the bottle, closing her eyes as she yanked the cork out and heard the distinctive pop, and then poured them both another glass.

Her legs felt wobbly, and she knew that he was frowning slightly, but she didn't care. The past week had been traumatic and she deserved to relax.

She was also feeling a little piqued. For the past two months she had told herself that what mattered most to her was that he should accept her professionally, but right now, right here, a part of her craved something else.

Instead of going back to the chair, she sat down on the sofa next to him. Was it her imagination, or did he take a swift, barely audible breath?

She looked sideways at him but his expression was bland.

'I don't think,' he murmured, 'that it's a very good idea for you to consume any more alcohol. What have you had to eat today?'

'Let's see...' She frowned. Her knee, she realised, with a little quiver of forbidden excitement, was nearly touching his thigh. 'I had some fruit for lunch and a bowl of soup earlier on.'

'And that's it?'

'And that's it,' she agreed, smiling at him. The lighting in the room was dim, and she looked at his face with surreptitious pleasure—the strong, smooth lines, the angle of his jaw, the sweep of his black hair.

She only realised that he was staring back at her when he said softly, 'All done?'

She didn't answer. There was a stillness in the room that made the hairs on the back of her neck stand on end. She reached out for her glass and immediately his hand snapped out and circled her wrist.

'I don't think so.' His voice was still soft but there was the hard edge of command in it.

She said irritably, 'Why did you bring me champagne if you didn't want me to drink it? You should have brought two bottles of orange squash.'

'I would have if I'd thought a bit harder about it,' he said, his hand still on her wrist.

Francesca shrugged and lowered her eyes, and he removed his hand.

'I think it's about time I left, don't you?'

'Why?'

He looked at her intently. 'I think you know the answer to that. Come on.' He stood up and she raised her eyes to his, confused.

'Where?'

'To the bedroom, my girl. I think you need to sleep this one off.'

Before she could utter a word of protest he bent down and picked her up, carrying her to the bedroom as if she weighed nothing. Of course, he was right. She was behaving in a crazy way, she knew that. With a little sigh she rested her head against his chest, hearing the steady beating of his heart, and half closed her eyes.

She couldn't remember having ever felt so frighteningly aware of anyone in her life before. But then, she thought, it wasn't as though her life had been cluttered with sexual exploits, was it? In fact, what she felt now stemmed from the dizzy Olympian heights of total inexperience.

She might have appeared on the surface to have enjoyed an uproarious few months, but she had never involved herself in all those things that seemed to go hand in hand with an uproarious life.

He placed her on the bed and switched on the side-light, and immediately the room was bathed in a warm glow. She lay back on the pillow and her eyes drifted across the dark wooden furniture, which looked so much nicer in this half-light than it did under the harsh light of day, when its cracks and grooves were so discernible.

Then her eyes drifted to his face.

'May I have a glass of water?' she asked, sitting up. 'The kitchen is…' She waved vaguely and he shot her a crooked smile.

'I don't think I need a map and compass to find my way to the kitchen.'

He left the room and returned before she had had much time to get her thoughts into order.

'Sit down,' she said, drinking the water, and after a little pause he sat next to her on the bed.

'How did you find this place?' he asked conversationally. He was such a formidably controlled person, she thought. What would it be like to see him out of control?

'Luck, aided and abetted by anger. I was so angry with Dad for involving me in his schemes, and with you.' Not that she felt angry now. She paused. 'Where do you live?'

'Hampstead. Not all that far from here, as a matter of fact.'

He began to stand up and she said quickly, not wanting him to go, 'Don't leave, not just yet.' In the silence her voice was almost a whisper and he sat back down, but with the expression of someone doing something against his better judgement.

Most men, she thought, would have jumped at the opportunity to be in a room with her. She had had enough blunt invitations before in her life to know that.

'Scared?' he asked. 'Is it the first time you've ever been on your own?'

'Yes,' she answered defiantly.

'Well, it's got to be done. Now, I think it's time you closed your eyes and went to sleep. Will the door self-lock behind me when I leave or do I need a key? I wouldn't like to leave you in here with the place wide open.'

'Why not?' She opened her eyes wide. 'Do you think someone might creep in in the dead of night and have his wicked way with me?'

'Or steal your television and video recorder, at any rate,' he said drily, raising his eyebrows. 'Better to be safe than sorry.'

'You needn't give me lectures. I've lived in London all my life! I know how to take care of myself.'

'You may have lived in London,' he said patiently, 'but you've been wrapped up in cotton wool. What would you do if a man broke into this place because you were stupid enough to forget to lock your door, or because you decided to keep the window open because it was a hot night?'

'What would anyone do?'

'I might have guessed you would answer a question with a question.' He laughed, and that irritated her.

'Do you think I'd be at any more of a disadvantage than if a burglar broke into your girlfriend's flat?' she asked, her mouth downturned at the corners.

'Imogen may look small and gullible, but she's far more streetwise than you are.'

'Because she comes from a different background?'

'This conversation,' he said, his voice cool, 'isn't getting us anywhere.'

'The least you could do is answer my question.' Her head was feeling considerably clearer now. In fact, her brain appeared to be working remarkably well.

'All right, then,' he said, with an edge of impatience. 'Yes. Growing up without a silver spoon in your mouth does mean that you have to develop a certain hardness, and that's a damn good protection. When there's no one around to make sure that the back door's shut you damn well realise soon enough that you've got to shut it yourself.'

'You're never going to forgive me for being the daughter of a rich man, are you?'

'I didn't realise that I had to forgive you for anything. You work hard and that's the bottom line.'

'I'm surprised you care whether you lock the outside door or not,' she muttered, irritated with herself for being perverse.

'I would care about leaving any woman alone in an open flat, especially in the state you're in.' He spoke evenly, making sure that she got the message.

'They're more likely to steer clear of me if they come

in and find me collapsed on the bed,' she said, biting back
the silly temptation to goad him into some response other
than complete, polite indifference.

'You think so?'

'What do you mean?' Her head was beginning to swim
a little again.

'Fishing, Francesca?' he asked, amused. 'Don't tell me
that I'm the first man to point out that you're a very attractive girl.' He patted her hand and glanced at his watch.

'Not attractive to you, though,' she said, and there was
silence.

'Do a few glasses of champagne usually have such an
effect on that tongue of yours?'

She shrugged. She felt as though she was on the edge
of something, as though some long-awaited event was
about to happen—although she couldn't work out what this
long-awaited thing was. She just knew that her pulses were
racing and her skin felt hot and tingly.

She raised her hand, and even though she felt muddled,
like someone floating softly above the clouds, a part of her
still knew that what she was about to do was insane.

She began unbuttoning her shirt, her eyes locked with
his. She had never realised that there were so many buttons
on this shirt. It seemed to take for ever but eventually she
reached the end, and she pulled aside the shirt, exposing
her breasts, full and round, her nipples erect. Her breathing
felt laborious.

'What the hell are you doing?' he asked on a sharp
breath, and she reached out and grasped his hand, guiding
it towards her aching breast. A sort of primeval instinct
seemed to have taken over, and as his hand made contact
with her skin she groaned and wriggled slightly.

He leaned forward, his eyes glittering in the semi-
darkened room, and his breathing, like hers, was quick and

uneven. It gave her a heady sense of power to see that some of that self-control had slipped.

When his mouth met hers she felt her body arch up against his, and her lips parted to allow the forceful entry of his tongue. His fingers had curled into her hair and he pulled her head back while, with his other hand, he cupped her breast.

He rubbed his thumb across her nipple and thousands of little electric currents seemed to fly through her. Through half-closed eyes she followed the progress of his dark head as his lips trailed downwards to her breasts, but she closed her eyes when his mouth encircled the swollen pink nipple and he began to suck it hard, pulling it into his mouth while his tongue licked the hardened tip.

Her eyes were still closed when he lifted his head to look at her, and it took a moment or two before she realised that he had straightened and was sitting up on the bed.

'What's wrong?' she asked, suddenly feeling freezing in the room now that the savage heat of his body had been taken away.

'You are,' he said curtly. 'Button up your shirt, for God's sake!'

She propelled herself into a sitting position and hurriedly pulled the gaping sides of her shirt together, hugging her arms around her.

He had stood up, and now that reality was revealing her humiliation in slow motion before her she wished that he would leave, but he didn't. He remained standing at the foot of the bed, staring down at her coldly.

'Was that the drink just then, Francesca, or do you make a habit of throwing yourself at whatever man happens to be around at the right time?'

His words cut into her like a whip and she raised her eyes to his. 'I do not sleep around!'

'Sure? That wasn't the impression I got just then.'

'I've never slept with a man in my life!'

That was the first time she had admitted it to anyone. Her friends, she knew, had all been involved in physical relationships, and it felt slightly odd that she was still a virgin. But she had never been seriously tempted.

Not, that was, until now, because she knew that if he had continued his love-making she would not have tried to stop him. She had wanted him with an intensity that was frightening, and, worse, she realised, with horrified mortification, she had wanted him for a long time now, and while the drink might have loosened her inhibitions it certainly hadn't provided the motivation.

He shook his head and raked his long fingers through his hair. 'You're looking at the wrong man if you want to broaden your experiences,' he said, leaning forward and resting the palms of his hands on the foot-board at the bottom of the bed.

She didn't say anything. She couldn't meet his eyes and she looked away in miserable confusion. Was that what she had wanted? No! Not in the way he had said. She hadn't wanted a man to broaden her experiences; she had wanted him.

'You're a good-looking girl,' he said tonelessly, 'and I admit that I was tempted to take what was on offer, but you're barking up the wrong tree. I might as well have this out with you once and for all. You aren't my type. No more, I suspect, than I am yours.'

'And what type do you see me with?' she asked lightly, even though her mouth felt cold and stiff.

'You're a child, Francesca. I have no time for children.'

They stared at each other in silence, then he spun round on his heels and walked out of the room. She heard the click of the outer door, and then she fell back on the bed and covered her face with a pillow.

Her mind was alive with torturous thoughts of how she had thrown herself at him. What had she hoped to achieve? she wondered. She remembered the feel of his hands on her breasts with a shudder of hot embarrassment.

When she had found out the real reason she had got the job with Oliver Kemp her pride had been crushed, but deep down, she realised, she had known that however she had managed to get the job she had succeeded in proving herself.

Now his rejection of her had shattered that bit of her pride which was irreparable. She had never been rejected in her life before, and what she felt now was a mixture of bewilderment, anger and hurt.

'I hate you,' she said aloud, and her words reverberated in the silence and then in her head, over and over and over, until sleep caught up with her and pulled a dark blind over her emotions.

CHAPTER FOUR

FRANCESCA felt tired and nervous on Monday morning when she walked into the office building. She had fallen asleep on Saturday with a gut-wrenching feeling of misery, and precisely the same feeling had stayed with her since.

She had made a decision, though. She might have thrown herself at Oliver Kemp, and he could make of that what he wanted, but there was no way that she would make that mistake again. Every time her mind replayed the scene she wanted to close her eyes and find herself a dark little corner where she could hide until her embarrassment faded.

And she didn't care what interpretation he chose to put on what had taken place. Let him go ahead and think that she had succumbed to the influence of drink, or even that she had wanted to lose her virginity to him for no better reason than that she had selfishly wanted the one man she knew she couldn't have, because she was little more than a spoiled, wilful child.

Just so long as he never suspected, even for a minute, that she was devastatingly attracted to him and had been long before she had even begun to put words to how she felt in his presence. That, she knew, he would find uproariously amusing. He might even—and she winced at this—be tempted to confide all in Imogen.

She met him, as luck would have it, in the lift, and as it slowly emptied he turned to her and said, his face unreadable, 'Feeling better?'

'Yes, thank you,' she answered, with a stiff smile. 'Yesterday my head felt as though someone was having a fine time jumping around inside it, but I took two aspirins and it soon felt better.'

He nodded, and as the lift stopped on their floor she said awkwardly, 'I want to apologise for Saturday night.'

He pushed open the office door to allow her past him, and even that brief brush by his body made her feel hot.

'No point talking about it—' he began in a cool voice.

She cut in swiftly, 'I think there is. I mean, I agree that there's no point in dwelling on it, but I'd just like to clear the air.'

'Go ahead, in that case.'

He looked at her and she wondered whether he was seeing her with her blouse open, her breasts exposed, straining towards him for the feel of his wet mouth. It took a great deal of effort not to wilt at the thought of that.

'I know you probably think the worst of me, but that sort of episode will never happen again. I can only think that the champagne must have gone to my head quicker than I thought, and I guess I was feeling a little maudlin, worrying about the way Dad and I parted company, wondering if I hadn't acted too recklessly.' It sounded the most rational excuse, and she made sure that her voice was very composed when she spoke.

'We all make mistakes,' he said, shrugging and turning away from her to riffle through the post on her desk.

'I'd fully understand,' she continued quietly, 'if you wanted me to leave.'

'Why should I?' He raised his light eyes to hers. 'I think the best thing is if we both relegate that unfortunate incident to the past, don't you?' He walked towards his office. 'Did you manage,' he asked, and she realised that he was already moving on, 'to finish working on that Peterborough file?'

She nodded and he said, taking it from her outstretched hand, 'The damned man's been on the phone again, wanting to know when we can complete our stock for him. I don't think he understands that phoning on an hourly basis isn't going to get things moving any quicker than they are already.'

She laughed dutifully at that, but she knew that already there had been a shift in their relationship.

Before the weekend they had been relaxed with one another. He had begun to take her competence for granted, which she had rather enjoyed, and although their private lives had remained huge, unspoken areas between them at least they had settled into a good working routine.

Now everything had changed. She was blindingly aware of him, and she knew that even though he had resumed his polite, distant manner things had been said, things had been done which had altered the surface calm.

It was as though something dangerous had been thrown into a pond, and although calm stillness had resettled on the water you knew that there was something there—something in the depths which would change the way you looked at that pond for ever.

He emerged at eleven o'clock to tell her that he would be out for the remainder of the day, and at twelve, when she was sitting in front of the computer, staring at the words on the screen, the telephone rang.

It was Imogen.

'I wonder if we can meet for lunch?' she said, and Francesca paled. Had he said something to his fiancée? She had hardly thought of the other woman on Saturday. It had been as if something had possessed her, leaving no room at all for thoughts of anyone else, and certainly not for the fact that he was involved with someone. Her face reddened now in guilty shame.

'Sure,' she said, clearing her throat, and listening while Imogen made arrangements as to where they could meet.

At five to one Francesca was waiting in anxious expectation at the wine bar which was only a stone's throw from the office. If Oliver had told his fiancée about what had happened, then she knew that she would have no alternative but to stop working for him.

She had been a thoughtless fool, she knew, and when Imogen finally arrived, ten minutes late, she was already feeling on the brink of confessing all and waiting for the axe to fall, knowing that it would be a well-deserved punishment.

But Imogen, smartly dressed in a navy blue suit and carrying a tiny black bag just large enough to hold her wallet and chequebook, did not look like a woman with an axe behind her back.

Francesca looked at the neat, intelligent figure and felt a sharp pang of bitter, unbridled jealousy, made all the worse by her knowledge that the qualities which Oliver saw in his fiancée were ones that she herself could never hope to achieve in a million years.

Her life, she realised, had been so uncomplicated before she'd met Oliver Kemp. She had skimmed merrily along the surface, like a water-skier flying across the waves, happily unaware that there were dangers under the sea waiting to engulf her.

After ten minutes her mouth ached from the strain of having to smile and chat, and she only surfaced into the conversation with any real interest when Imogen told her that she needed some advice.

'What about?' Francesca asked, surprised, and Imogen looked at her thoughtfully.

'Clothes. I want to change my wardrobe a bit and I

thought, Who better to ask than you? You're such a gorgeous dresser.'

'Why do you want to change your wardrobe?' Francesca asked, bewildered. 'In your position—'

'Oh, I know that. Power-suits for work. The problem is I can't seem to break out of the power-dressing ethos.' She laughed, as if astonished at her desire to do so. 'I need some bright colours, some variety.'

'Why? Doesn't Oliver love you the way you are?' That took a great deal of effort, and she felt quite sick after she had said it.

'Oh, a change is as good as a rest, don't you think?' Imogen answered ambiguously, smiling and sipping some of her orange juice.

'He may not think so,' Francesca said, with a tight little smile.

'Then again,' Imogen murmured, 'he might be pleasantly surprised.' But she had lowered her eyes and, with a little shrug, Francesca chatted briefly about where she shopped, giving her names of people who would happily kit her out in whatever she wanted.

Her mind conjured up images of the other woman dressed seductively, images of Oliver finding that a pleasant surprise, images of them making love, and it was with relief when she parted company from Imogen outside the wine bar.

Over the next two days Francesca kept her head down, barely glanced in the direction of Oliver, and tried desperately to reason with herself.

What she felt for him, she told herself—this terrible pull—was foolish and pointless, and, having recognised that, she should be able to shrug it off to experience, but every time he came near her her body went into overdrive.

When he leaned by her to show her something she had to keep her hands tightly clenched by her sides so that he couldn't see how much they were trembling. When he spoke to her she had to make sure that her eyes didn't meet his because she didn't want him to read the message waiting there for him.

'What's the matter with you?' he asked on the Wednesday evening as she was about to leave. He had called her into his office to go through some files with her, and he sat back in his chair and looked at her carefully through narrowed eyes.

'I feel a bit ill,' she replied quickly. 'I think I must be coming down with something. There's a lot of flu going around.'

'You're working too hard,' he said without emphasis. 'Do you ever have a lunch break?'

'Occasionally. I met your fiancée for lunch the other day. We went to the wine bar down the road.'

'Yes. She told me.' He didn't appear to want to pursue that.

'She wanted some advice on clothes, so she came to me. Who better? Anyone can see that my forte is knowing how to put an outfit together.' She couldn't help it. Her voice was laced with bitterness, and she could have kicked herself for the little slip in her well-maintained façade.

He frowned. 'If that's what you think of yourself then it won't be too difficult for the rest of the world to fall in with your opinion, will it?'

'I suppose not.' She laughed shortly and stood up. 'If it's all right, I think I'll call it a day now. Unless you want these letters typed urgently?'

'They can wait.' His eyes were still on her and she nervously looked away and moved towards the door, half expecting him to call her back, half wanting it, in fact, but he didn't, and when she looked back at him, his head was downbent reading reports.

She felt so angrily miserable as she let herself out of his office that she was almost happy when she looked up and saw Brad Robinson by her desk.

She had seen him often enough over the months, and she had become quite accustomed to his brand of outrageous flirtation. She still smilingly disregarded all of it, but she no longer found it as oppressive and disagreeable as she had done the very first time she had met him.

It had helped, she supposed, that, contrary to her initial judgements, he wasn't married. He still thought himself a creation handmade for the benefit of the opposite sex, but at least there wasn't some poor woman in the background, building a life around him.

'You look terrible,' he said, his eyes sweeping over her appraisingly as they always did.

'I feel terrible,' she answered, clearing her desk and automatically pushing him off his perch by the computer terminal. 'My head aches, my back aches, my eyes ache.'

'Would an all-over body massage be the thing?' He flexed his fingers and shot her a wolfish, enquiring look which brought a reluctant grin to her lips.

'Well,' she said, not looking at him but still grinning, 'that certainly beats all the usual clichés I've heard from you in the past, Brad.'

'Doesn't it?' he asked, giving that some thought. 'Perhaps I could incorporate it in my repertoire.'

Before she could comment on that one he had moved behind her, and she felt his hands on her shoulders, his thumbs pressing against her muscles.

'Feel good?' he asked in her ear, and she had to admit that it did.

'Just so long as those hands of yours don't develop any

wanderlust,' she said, tilting her head back and half closing her eyes.

'I'll try to keep them in check,' he said, and she didn't have to see him to know that he was grinning. 'But they can sometimes be bad little boys when it comes to the opposite sex.'

'Oh, good grief,' she murmured, flexing her shoulders. Neither of them heard the connecting door open. When Oliver spoke his voice was like the crack of a whip, and they sprang apart.

'Are you here for something in particular?' he asked Brad, his mouth drawn into a tight line. He stood where he was and folded his arms, and every muscle in his body was taut with suppressed aggression. 'Because if you are then say so, and if you're not you can get back to your office and do what you're so lavishly paid to do.'

'We were just on our way out,' Francesca said, her colour high, and he rounded on her.

'No. You've got it wrong. Mr Robinson here is on his way out, and you, my girl—in my office. Now!'

He spun round on his heels, and she could feel her anger mounting as she followed him into the office and closed the door behind her. 'That was unnecessary!' she burst out, watching him angrily from a distance, alarmed by the black fury on his face.

'Don't you tell me what's necessary and what's unnecessary in my own damn company! Do you understand me?'

'He only came for a chat before we left,' she mumbled, and he strode towards her and took her by the shoulders. She felt the grip of his fingers and winced in pain.

'This is not a playground,' he muttered, his black brows drawn together in a harsh frown, 'and I don't pay my employees to cavort during office hours! Is that clear?'

'Brad always flirts,' she said, looking away guiltily because she knew that she should have discouraged him, and would have if she hadn't been feeling so low. 'You told me that yourself when I first joined.'

'That's no excuse to abuse my trust, is it?' he snarled. 'I don't damned well expect to find you fornicating on the office floor just because you imagine that you can get away with it.'

Her head shot up. 'I'd hardly call it that!' she snapped, her colour high. 'And you're hurting me!'

He released her abruptly but he didn't move. He remained where he was, his hands thrust into his pockets.

'And you expect to be taken seriously?' he asked, with a sneer in his voice. 'If you insist on behaving like an adolescent, then please tell me, and I'll gladly hand you back over to your father, and he can find himself another school of correction for you—debt or no debt.'

Their eyes met and, oddly, he was the first to look away. He stalked across to the window, then turned back to look at her.

'It won't happen again,' she muttered, realising that she was shaking all over.

'Good. Because if it does then you're out, and so is he.'

'You wouldn't!' She looked at him, appalled by the savagery of the threat. 'He's a good salesman. You said so yourself!'

'You heard me.' He turned away and stared out of the window, waiting for her to leave, and she did, after a moment's silence.

She had never seen him so furious. What had got into him? Had he exploded over that little incident because he was looking around for an excuse to get rid of her? she wondered. He might have told her that they could put her stupid, childish indiscretion behind them and continue working together, but had he really meant it?

She was still frowning, turning over the problem in her mind as she let herself into her block of flats, and in the gloomy entrance hall she didn't see the umbrella lying on the floor. One minute she was hurtling towards the staircase and the next minute she was on the floor. She stood up and then sat back down and began massaging her ankle.

It hurt like mad, and she eyed the offending umbrella with loathing. Eventually she tentatively tried to stand up again and found that she could just hobble up to her flat, with much clinging to the banister, and only very slowly.

The only bright spot was that her throbbing ankle did succeed in diverting her thoughts from Oliver slightly. She prepared herself a light supper, which turned out to be a one-hour job and left her feeling exhausted. At eight she telephoned her doctor, a family friend, who asked her a series of detailed questions on the phone, told her that she had just sprained the ankle, that the pain would subside but that she could take aspirin if she found it helped.

'Thanks very much, Dr Wilkins,' she said tartly. 'I already feel a lot better.' He laughed at that, told her that he would telephone her in the morning, and to have a good night's sleep.

It didn't feel a whole lot better in the morning, and with a sigh of resignation she phoned through to the office and connected immediately with Oliver on his direct line.

'I'm afraid I can't come in,' she said, twisting the telephone cord and wondering how his presence could fill the flat when he wasn't even in the room.

'Why not?' No words of concern, no sympathetic cluckings. Had she expected otherwise?

'I've twisted my ankle,' she admitted, 'I can hardly walk.'

'Careless,' he said briefly. 'Especially as I need to go over those pending files with you.'

'I really do apologise, Mr Kemp,' Francesca said in a syrupy voice, scowling down the line. 'Next time I'll try to plan my accidents for more opportune moments.'

'That would be useful,' he agreed, and she gritted her teeth together in frustration. 'However, all's not lost. I'll drop by this evening after work, say about six-thirty.'

'Drop by…?' she asked, horrified at the prospect of that, but he had already hung up, and she heard the dead dialling sound of the phone in her ear with annoyance.

She spent the remainder of the day in a state of tense anticipation. Rupert's appearance at lunchtime was almost irritating. She hadn't seen him for a while, and now she was beginning to find him trivial. He was amusing, but sometimes she didn't want to be amused, and he would never understand that. For him life was one long, enjoyable, never-ending game, but that got tiring after a while.

She found herself looking at her watch more than once, and when he stood up to leave he said, sharply for him, 'Sorry I disturbed you by dropping by, Frankie. When I phoned your office and I was told about your ankle I thought you might appreciate the company.'

'I'm sorry, Rupert,' she said, meaning it. 'But I've got a lot on my mind,' she added, meaning that too. Rather fervently.

'So have I,' he surprised her by saying, and he hesitated. He was thinking about whether to confide in her, she realised. It was the first time she had ever seen so much as a frown cross his amiable face, and she immediately felt ashamed that she hadn't been paying more attention to what he had been saying.

'Anything you want to talk about?' she asked, giving

him her undivided attention, and he shrugged, with the same hesitation in his manner.

'Not really,' he finally said. 'Usual woman troubles.'

'Usual? Rupert, you never have woman troubles.'

He laughed, and she realised what she hadn't noticed before, that he had been worried when he had first arrived.

'I know,' he agreed, nodding. 'Bit of a shame I'm having to find out about them now, at my ripe old age.'

But that was as far as she got, because he left without really saying much more to her, and very soon she forgot all about the conversation.

Of course, as she might have expected, Oliver didn't arrive until after seven, by which time tension had given way to anger. Having decided, she thought mutinously, that he could invade her flat just because he needed some work doing, he now thought that he could walk in at whatever time he pleased.

When she heard the sharp knock on the door she hobbled across and pulled it open, her mouth tightly set.

He eyed her very slowly, from foot to head and back to swollen foot, then picked her up bodily, ignoring her protests.

'There,' he said, depositing her on the chair, then removing his coat. It was raining outside—a steady drumming beat against the window panes. 'I've brought us food,' he said, and she noticed the brown bag. 'Chinese. I hope you like it.'

Something in his manner alarmed her, although she couldn't quite put her finger on it. It was like trying to reach for a shadow—something elusive but disturbing all the same. She wondered whether she wasn't imagining it because she had been living in a state of such heightened awareness recently.

'That was very thoughtful of you,' she said awkwardly, remembering how disastrous his last appearance at her flat had been.

'I didn't think that you'd get around to cooking in your state,' he pointed out, vanishing into the kitchen and emerging a couple of minutes later with two plates and some cutlery.

She watched, nervously silent, as he fished the little foil containers from the bag and undid lids.

'Doesn't look very appetising, does it?' he asked, handing her the plate, and she smiled.

'Smells good, though.' She looked at him from under her lashes, feeding on his devastating male sexuality like a foodaholic greedily looking at a plate of food. It was a terrible, forbidden pleasure but she couldn't resist it.

Now that she had acknowledged her attraction to him everything about him was an impact on her senses—the strong lines of his face, the power of his body, the way his black hair curled against the nape of his neck. She took it all in, adding it to her little store of images which had swelled and multiplied over the months without her even realising it.

She looked at him when she thought that her hunger would go unnoticed, but she felt like a thief in the night, stealing something that didn't belong to her.

'How are you settling in?' he asked neutrally. 'Any regrets?'

In between mouthfuls of food she chatted to him, answered his questions, told herself that the only threat to her peace of mind was herself. And he was, not all that surprisingly, easy to talk to. He had the rare gift of being able to listen attentively, and after a while she found herself talking to him more freely than she would have expected.

Why, though, was he being so nice, so charming? The little question kept floating into her head intermittently, but she chose to disregard it.

'You know all about me, though,' she said eventually, putting her plate on the table in front of her. 'You know my background,' she said, 'and heaven only knows what else, thanks to my father.'

'So I do,' he agreed smoothly.

'So why don't we get down to work? If you leave the dishes in the sink I can do them later.'

He nodded, and for the next hour they went through files. She deciphered her shorthand jottings, made notes of things that she needed to do as soon as she got into the office, and when they were finished he sat back and said, 'In case you're wondering why I came over here, the reason is that I shall be abroad for the next three weeks. Urgent business.'

'Ah.' That made sense. He had needed to discuss work because he wouldn't be around, and she didn't know whether the news of his absence from the office filled her with relief or disappointment.

'I'll be in touch, of course, every day, but you'll have to carry on without me. Can you manage?'

'What do you think?'

He looked at her thoughtfully. 'I have no doubts that you can,' he murmured, giving her a crooked smile that sent little shivers through her. 'Does it feel good to you, knowing that I was wrong about you? I'm not usually wrong in my judgements of people, but I have to admit your work has been superb.'

'Is that the sound of a man eating humble pie?' she asked, and he laughed.

'I think I'll pass on that question. Humble pie tends to give me indigestion.'

He stood up and she thought that he was going to leave, but he wasn't. He went into the kitchen, fetched them both some coffee and handed a cup to her.

'Thank you,' she said, taking the cup, surprised. 'I wouldn't have thought that you had a domesticated streak in you. First the food, now this.'

'Making a cup of coffee isn't quite beyond me,' he replied drily, sitting back down and raking his fingers through his hair. 'I can even do a halfway decent meal when pressed.'

'I suppose you had to when you were at university,' Francesca commented, not looking at him.

'And before. My mother was quite ill before she died. I had to do all the household chores, in between studying like crazy. I became a dab hand at wielding a vacuum cleaner and revising statistics at the same time.'

She laughed and wondered fleetingly how a man could be so hard, so aggressive and yet so witty when he chose to be.

'It must have been hard,' she said, 'being on your own.'

'I learnt pretty quickly how to stand on my own two feet.' He shrugged. 'It's no bad lesson to learn.'

Here we go, she thought. Here come the veiled criticisms.

'I don't suppose there are too many people who would disagree with that,' she said lightly. 'Not when they see what a success can be made from it.'

'Success is a dubious beast,' he murmured, and this time when he looked at her his eyes held hers for a fraction longer than was necessary. 'Success, sadly, breeds suspicion. The more money you make, the narrower becomes the circle of people whom you can trust. You must have found that.'

'Not really,' she answered, thinking about it.

'Because you lived in an exalted world far removed from reality.' It was more a statement of fact rather than a question.

'It wasn't one I chose,' she pointed out, not willing to spoil the pleasant atmosphere between them. She stood up to carry the cups into the kitchen and to stretch her muscles, which felt as though they were slowly seizing up on her, and as she bent down to retrieve his cup from the ground he reached out and caught her wrist in his hand.

'You shouldn't be moving about,' he said softly.

Her heart began to thud. She felt that familiar excitement course through her and she tried to look at him calmly, without letting her body dictate her responses.

'M-my ankle feels m-much better already,' she stammered, and he pulled her gently down onto the sofa next to him.

'Let me have a look at it,' he said, and she looked at him in panic.

'There's nothing to look at,' she protested. 'It's just a bit bruised.'

'How did you do it? I never asked.'

He gently lifted her leg onto his lap and shoved up her long skirt so that her ankle was exposed. It was ridiculous but she felt as exposed and vulnerable as a Victorian lady being stripped. She also felt confused. Why was he doing this, behaving like this? She remembered his cold words of contempt when she had thrown herself at him, and she pulled her leg, but he held it firmly in place.

'Well?' he asked, looking up at her, and she had to think before she remembered what his question had been in the first place.

'Oh, I tripped over an umbrella.'

'Novel.' He bent his head to inspect the ankle, and very carefully he stroked it with his hand.

'What are you doing?' Was that her voice? It sounded like a terrified squeak.

He ignored that. 'What did the doctor say?'

'It should be better tomorrow, or else definitely by the day after.'

'I'm glad to hear it.' He gave her a slow, lazy smile and she finally realised what her subconscious had been telling her all along. Oliver Kemp was flirting with her.

It was so unexpected that it was almost shocking. She glanced down at her entwined fingers and felt rather than saw his eyes roaming over her.

She felt oddly at sea with this frank appraisal from a man who had hardly so much as glanced in her direction in the past, and, when he had, had done so with the indifference of a man who saw no sexuality in the woman at whom he was looking.

There was no rush of longing on her part, though. She had flung herself at him with the naïve optimism of inexperience, and now that same inexperience, when faced with this sophisticated game of seduction, was pulling her back. She felt bewildered and defensive.

She gave another tug of her foot and he asked in a low, casual voice, 'Do you want me to leave?'

There was silence—a silence so profound that every little sound in the room was amplified a million times over. The gentle spitting of the rain against the window-pane became a drum roll; the ticking of the clock on the mantelpiece sounded like a time bomb about to go off.

'What time is it?' she heard herself ask for want of anything better to say, and there was dry irony in his eyes when they rested on her.

'Time to leave or time to stay. Tell me which.'

'I don't understand what's going on,' she said evenly. 'When you were last here—'

'You had had too much to drink,' he said, but she had the uneasy, fleeting feeling that he wasn't telling the whole truth.

She lifted her leg from his lap and rested it gently on the ground, and then stared at it in apparent fascination.

She was so aware of the man sitting next to her that she could hardly breathe. Her blonde hair hung across her face like a curtain, hiding her expression, for which she was glad because the last thing she needed was to have him read the thoughts flitting across her face.

'Why,' he asked, sweeping her hair back with his hand, 'don't you look at me?'

He didn't move his hand. He curled his fingers against the nape of her neck and she reluctantly faced him.

'Is it a stupid question to ask whether you've been drinking?' She attempted a light laugh which emerged as something of a choked noise.

'Very stupid.'

Now that she had her eyes firmly fixed on his face she found that she couldn't drag her gaze away. 'I'm afraid I'm missing something here,' she whispered. 'None of this makes any sense.'

'Some things don't,' he murmured, and she had that feeling again, as though there was a thread of meaning behind his words which she couldn't quite comprehend.

'Are you scared?' he asked, and she didn't say anything. 'Do you,' he continued, 'want me to make love to you, Francesca Wade?'

CHAPTER FIVE

FRANCESCA wasn't so green that she hadn't understood the signals coming from Oliver, but now that the words were out of his mouth, now that he was staring at her with that glittering intensity in his eyes, she found that she couldn't think at all.

'W-what?' she stammered.

He didn't repeat what he had said. He just continued looking at her and the blood rushed to her head with such force that she thought she was going to faint.

'What about Imogen?' she asked faintly, and that drew a short, humourless smile to his lips.

'Imogen and I have decided that we need to think things over.'

'You mean you've decided to split with her? Why?'

'Why do people ever split up?' he asked, with a hint of impatience in his voice now, as though they were drifting from the matter at hand into waters that were only marginally relevant and certainly did not warrant much explanation.

'You and she were so well suited,' Francesca said, frowning and trying to read all the meanings behind this revelation—meanings hidden underneath his silence.

'I didn't realise you knew me so well,' he drawled with amused sarcasm.

Know you well? she thought suddenly, looking across at him. I don't know you at all.

'You still haven't answered my question,' he said softly, but before she could say anything he raised his hand. 'No, don't answer. Not yet.' Then he leaned across to her and she closed her eyes before his mouth touched hers. She felt the warmth of his lips as they took hers in a kiss that lingered persuasively, then, as her mouth parted, hungrily moved in a kiss that made her feel as if she was drowning.

She groaned and tried to pull back.

'What's the matter?' he asked, releasing her, but only slightly so that, although she could speak, the sheer power of his sexuality still kept her in its grip.

'You don't find me attractive,' she said unsteadily. Her mouth obligingly said one thing, but her body said another, because she still grasped his shirt, and she knew that however many questions were unanswered, however many doubts she had that what she was doing was right the pull she felt for him was just too strong.

'Maybe I find you too attractive,' he murmured, his eyes veiled. He trailed his finger along her spine and she felt her body begin to melt.

This time when he bent to kiss her her answer to his question was there in her response. He held the sides of her head with his hands, pushing her back.

'I want to hear you tell me that this is what you want,' he whispered roughly into her ear, and she felt the tingling of his warm breath with a shudder of deep excitement.

'It's what I want,' she said, in barely a whisper. It's what I have wanted for so long now, she could have added. It's what I've wanted all my life.

He swept her up and carried her towards the bedroom, kicking open the door with his foot, and this time when he lay her down on the bed there was naked desire in his eyes.

He hadn't bothered to switch on the bedroom light, but he had left the door to the small sitting room open so that the light filtered into the room from there, giving the bedroom a shadowy, mosaic feel.

'You're so damned young,' he muttered, and she anxiously wondered whether this marked the beginning of a retreat.

'I'm not,' she denied. 'I'm not young and I know what I'm doing.'

'Oh, I'm not talking about your age,' he said. He was sitting next to her, and he placed his hands on either side of her supine body, so that she was in a cage. She reached out and put her hands on his arms.

'What, then?' she asked, trying to be calm, already trying to step over the pain of his leaving, if that was what he was going to do.

'You're very ingenuous,' he said. 'Not at all what I imagined when your father first described you. Oh, you have the social *savoir-faire* that comes to a woman born into wealth, but underneath you're like a child.'

'And you're so experienced,' she said huskily. 'You sound like an old man, but you're not, are you?'

'Sometimes I feel as though I am.'

'Old and with a string of lovers behind you?' She made herself laugh, but she wasn't laughing inside. Inside, her heart was twisting with jealousy at all those imaginary lovers that had passed through his life.

'Not a string,' he murmured, stroking her face with his finger, tracing the contours of her cheek-bones, her eyebrows, the outline of her lips. His touch was light and feathery, and she knew that her breathing had quickened and that the strings deep inside her were becoming more urgent.

'I've never made a habit of moving from one warm body to another.'

'No?' she asked, lowering her eyes.

'No.' He laughed under his breath.

'But I'm sure you must have had countless offers,' she said.

'Oh, countless. Any more questions?' He laughed softly again, then bent to kiss her neck and she wrapped her arms around him, pulling him towards her.

If there were any more questions, she couldn't think of them. Come to that, she couldn't think of anything at all. Thinking was proving to be beyond her.

He pushed up her shirt, pulling it over her head, then he stood up and she watched, feverish, as he slowly took off his clothes, never taking his eyes off her face, enjoying her frank appreciation of his body.

Whatever he had said about not having had a string of lovers, there was no doubt that she was watching a man well-versed in the art of making love.

His nudity made her gasp with sudden, wild yearning. Physically he was perfect, as lean and muscular as an athlete, even though she knew that he didn't do any exercise—he didn't have the time.

He slipped onto the bed next to her, but before she could begin removing her long skirt, he asked, 'Are you protected?'

'Protected? Protected against what?' She couldn't imagine what he was talking about. What should she be protected against? The only protection she could think of was when she had started travelling abroad at the age of six and had had vaccinations.

'What do you think?' he murmured. 'Pregnancy, of course.'

'Of course.' Her brain engaged and she said swiftly, 'Yes, I am.'

'Good.' Even as he said that he unzipped her skirt and she wriggled free of it, but when she went to slip off her lacy underwear he put his hand over hers and said roughly, 'Not yet.'

Not yet? It was agonising having any clothes on, even underwear. She wanted him so badly.

He lowered his head against her breasts, sucking them, playing with them, rolling her nipple between his fingers, then he moved his hand lower, against the flat planes of her stomach, and she parted her legs with a little groan of pleasure.

When he cupped her underneath the briefs with his hand she felt her body shudder, and she moved spontaneously against him, moaning as his fingers found the moist depths of her femininity.

But he wouldn't let her reach that pinnacle of satisfaction. He slowed the rhythm of his strokes and slipped off her underwear, then guided her hand to his throbbing masculinity.

She turned on her side to face him, but he gently pushed her flat, bending over her so that his exploring mouth could follow the seductive path of his fingers. His tongue teased and she closed her eyes, feeling her body lift to regions which she had never dreamt possible.

When he finally entered her any momentary pain was swamped by her sheer need for him, and the mounting rhythm of his movements sent her spinning at last beyond imagination, beyond thought.

In fact, thought processes only began once again when they were lying next to one another. Did the earth move for you too? she wanted to ask him. Did lightning strike? All those clichés which she had heard about and read about now seemed to possess an accuracy which she would never have thought possible. Was physical attraction *this* strong? she asked herself, vaguely perturbed.

She didn't ask him, though. In fact, she said with utter banality, 'What time do you leave tomorrow?'

'Early,' he replied, stroking her hair. 'Why?'

'No reason.' She swept her hand along his side and wondered whether he would miss her. She thought not. He might not believe in casual sex, but that didn't mean that he considered her his destiny, did it? That didn't mean that he loved her.

She felt a momentary jolt of shock. What had love to do with anything? she wondered, trembling. Nothing? Or everything?

'What happens when you get back, Oliver?' she asked hurriedly, feeling a bit like someone whose boat had capsized and who was trying desperately to clamber back on, and he frowned.

'What happens about what?'

'About us?'

His eyes narrowed but he continued stroking her. 'I run my business; you work for me; we make love.'

'You make it sound so simple.'

'Isn't it?'

'Nothing in life is simple,' she said, and he gave her a slow, amused smile.

'You sound like an adult now,' he murmured.

She said in a sharper voice than she had intended, 'I am an adult.'

'Then as an adult you should know how it stands between us without my having to spell it out. I'm not looking for commitment.' There was a hard edge in his voice when he said that.

'Just fun.'

'It's a philosophy you should be well acquainted with.'

She couldn't begin to put into words how ill acquainted she was with any philosophy of the sort. She might have spent months avoiding responsibility and having fun, but none of it had involved sex.

'I guess so,' she said lightly, and was it her imagination or did his body relax? 'Was it just fun with Imogen?'

'Imogen was—is—a very special person,' he said thoughtfully. 'On paper we were the ideal couple, which just goes to prove that nothing in life is a certainty. We were on the same wavelength, our experiences had been pretty much the same, we were made from similar moulds, you might say—but in the end it wasn't enough.'

'Are you bitter about it?' she asked, but tentatively, because she felt rather than knew that at any point when he decided that her questions were none of her business he would switch off.

'Why should I be bitter?' And again there was that hard edge in his voice. 'It happened. And, like all experiences, I've learnt a lesson from this one.'

'Which is?' She had no idea why she bothered to ask the question, because she knew what he was going to say even before he said it.

'That marriage is something for other people.' He laughed, but there was no humour behind the laughter. 'Now, aren't there more interesting things we could be doing, apart from talking?'

He cradled her breast in his hand and her body made the decision before her mind even had time to think about it. She sighed, nodding languidly, and this time when he laughed there was warm amusement there.

'You're a passionate little creature, aren't you?' He aroused her nipple into hardness, and she needed no asking to take his manhood in her hands, to tease him as he was teasing her. When hunger began to replace the lazy amusement in his eyes she felt a surge of power that she could do this to him.

Their love-making this time round was slow and easy, and less one-sided. They built each other up with caresses that seemed to have no beginning and no end.

Where did this wanton passion spring from? she wondered, but she knew the answer to that one. The answer had been lurking just out of reach, but always there—the uninvited guest waiting to come in. Now the guest had entered, and Francesca knew with shuddering certainty why she had made love to him.

Underneath the physical pull was something stronger, more powerful, less manageable—a burning love, a dark fire that would not go back whence it came. She could have fought against simple desire, but what weapons did she have against what she was feeling now? And did she, she wondered tremulously, want any?

She lay on him, letting her full breasts hang temptingly to his mouth, smiling when he caught one provocative nipple and began suckling on it while his hands gripped her waist, almost encircling it completely. When she eased her body onto him she found a rhythm of her own and arched back as the rhythm took her again and again to sexual fulfilment.

It was only later, when he said that it was time for him to go, that she looked at the clock by the bed and saw that it was after midnight.

'I've got to pack,' he said, standing up. He looked at her. 'I'm going to have a quick shower. I'd invite you along, but if I did I'm not sure I'd make it out in time to do any packing at all before I leave.'

She smiled drowsily and lay back, hearing the distant sound of the shower going and letting her thoughts take their course, stray wherever they wanted to.

He didn't want commitment. That should have sent her

spinning into despair and regret, but it didn't. How could she regret what had happened between them? All he wanted was uninvolved fun, and, much as she craved something way beyond that, part of her had already decided—when, she couldn't say—that she would take what he was offering, because the alternative was to walk away from him and she didn't know if she could do that.

In the end she would be hurt. That was as inevitable as day following night, but at least her pain would come in the wake of something which she had spent her life waiting for.

Maybe, she thought, if she hadn't slept with him she could have walked away, but now she had given too much.

She looked at him as he emerged out of the shower, drying his hair roughly with a towel, and just wished that he wasn't about to disappear from the face of the earth— or as good as anyway—for three weeks. Three weeks was such a long time, but it couldn't be helped.

He was opening a subsidiary and it would need time to get sorted out, he had told her. The preliminaries would have to be done by him, because when he worked he worked to a level of perfection which he couldn't trust anyone else to achieve.

That, she knew, was why he had done so well in life. He never took short cuts and he never accepted anything less than the best. Was that what had finally made things fail between him and Imogen? She watched as he slipped on his clothes and wondered whether he had expected that relationship to attain a level which was out of reach.

When he came to stand by the bed he bent down and kissed her lightly on her forehead—a goodbye-and-sweet-dreams kind of kiss that made her smile.

'I'll be in touch every day,' he said, and she nodded.

'What shall I do if I run into a problem I can't handle?'

'Send me a fax. If it's really urgent I guess I can return, but I'd rather get this thing over and done with, without breaking off in between.'

She desperately wanted to ask him if he would miss her, but already she knew what questions were permissible and which ones weren't, and that one was definitely in the no-go zone.

He left quietly, and she lay in bed for a long time, awake and empty, thinking that she would never be able to sleep, but eventually she did.

When she awoke the following morning it was nearly ten o'clock and, after some internal debate, she decided to take another day off so that her ankle could heal up completely before she went in.

It seemed strange when she did make it into work the following week to be in that office on her own. She had become accustomed to listening out for him, to knowing that he was close by.

After three days she realised that the only thing that kept her going was his daily phone calls. Then his voice seemed to bring him into the same room with her.

'Missing me?' he had asked lightly down the line the day before.

She had laughed as lightly as he had spoken and said, 'Of course! There have been a lot of queries I would much rather you had dealt with.'

She wasn't going to show him how deep her feelings for him ran, even in the occasional passing remark, and a small part of her optimistically hoped that in time fun would develop into something else. She didn't like dwelling on the thought that it might not, that he might tire of her the way a child tired of a toy that had outlived its welcome.

You didn't have to be a genius to know that any relationship that existed solely on sex would eventually run out of steam, and as far as he was concerned sex was the only thing that drew him to her. She certainly was not his ideal woman the way Imogen had been, and if that had failed what chance did they stand?

But she avoided thinking along those lines. Instead she told herself that nothing in life was beyond reach, not if you tried hard enough.

She was clearing her desk to go home, two weeks after he had left—each day mentally ticked off on her calendar—when Helen walked into the office.

Francesca had not seen the other girl for quite some time—at least five weeks or so—even though she occasionally met her in the cloakroom, which served two floors. At times like that she made obligatory polite conversation, because bad atmospheres were not a good idea in an office environment, but that was all—a 'Hello, how are you? Oliver will have that stuff you phoned about for you later today,' and then a quick escape.

Now she looked at the other girl warily, keeping her hands busy with her tidying, letting it be clear that she was about to leave so that Helen would not invite herself into conversation.

It didn't work. Helen looked at her with her hard eyes and said brightly, 'How are you coping without your big, bad boss?'

'Fine.' A bit more meaningful tidying.

'Rumours have been floating around the building about him...' Helen picked up a pen and scrutinised it.

'Really?' Francesca answered, her body tensing even though she kept her voice casually uninterested.

'Really.' The pen was deposited and Helen gave her a long stare.

Her face, as usual, was heavily made up, which made her eyes look even more alarming, and she was dressed inappropriately in a very short black skirt and a long-sleeved top which left precious little to the imagination. The etiquette of office dressing had obviously passed her by, because Francesca had never seen her in anything that did not look as though it should be worn in a nightclub instead of at a desk. No doubt the men appreciated that, and no doubt Helen didn't object in the slightest.

'Rumour has it that he and his girlfriend are no more.'

'Is that a fact?' The casualness in her voice was slipping a little. She didn't want to discuss any of this, not at all.

'Sure is. Rumour also has it that the reason they hit the rocks was because she found someone else.'

'Oh? People shouldn't believe everything that's said.'

'Seen, actually. At a nightclub. With some fair-haired guy.'

'Fair-haired guy?' Francesca asked sickly. She was beginning to sound parrot-like, she knew, repeating everything as though she were hard of hearing. 'Who told you that?'

'Friend of a friend. I kind of wished that I had been there. I can't imagine Miss Imogen High and Mighty living it up, can you?'

Yes, Francesca thought, I can.

'This friend of a friend knew someone who knew the guy she was with. Vaguely. Rupert something or other. Old flame of yours, I believe.'

The heavily made-up eyes were slits, and Francesca nodded without saying anything. It hadn't even crossed her mind that Rupert had not been in touch with her for weeks.

It hadn't crossed her mind because there had been so much else there filling it up.

Now she remembered the last time she had seen him, when he had mentioned in passing that he was having woman problems. No wonder he had felt reluctant about going into details. How could he have when the problem was a bit too near home for his liking?

'I wonder how Oliver took it?' Helen asked herself.

Without thinking Francesca said, 'He didn't seem too crushed.' The minute the words were out she felt herself go bright red.

'He's been confiding in you?'

'I have to go now, Helen. Was there anything else you wanted?'

'He's not the sort to confide, not from what I've seen of him. So how come you know about his personal life?' She followed Francesca to the coat rack like a bloodhound on the scent, and Francesca kept her head averted, putting on her coat. Eventually, though, she had to turn round, and when she did Helen asked sharply, 'Have you slept with him?'

Instead of protesting, which was what she should have done, she hesitated, and that brief hesitation was enough. Helen looked at her viciously and nodded.

'Decided to get in there while the going was good, did you? You little bitch!'

'Don't be silly,' Francesca said weakly, knowing that it was too late, that her moment's silence had cost her dear.

'Took advantage because he was on his own? Or did he decide that you would do, you would tide him through a bad night?'

'I'm going.' Francesca began walking towards the door, hoping that the other girl would not pursue her down to the ground floor, because in a lift there would be no escape.

'I should have known that that butter-wouldn't-melt-in-my-mouth face of yours was a put-on,' she spat out, and Francesca saw with distaste that the venom there was a case of the cat thinking that its cream had been heartily lapped up in its absence.

'I'll make sure that everyone within a twenty-mile radius knows what's going on,' she said, with a cold smile, and Francesca stopped in her tracks.

She hadn't wanted this argument, but now that she was embroiled in it, she felt angry blood rush to her head. 'If you do,' she said quietly, 'I'll make sure that Oliver knows exactly who started the gossip, and you'll soon find yourself out of a job.'

She had never threatened anyone in her life before, and she was shaking like a leaf. They stared at each other wordlessly for a few seconds, and she could tell that Helen was digesting that, wondering whether spreading her story was worth her job—her no doubt highly paid job.

'I'll make sure that you pay,' she contented herself with saying. 'Somehow.'

The lift came and Francesca hopped in, pressing the ground-floor button and breathing a sigh of relief when she realised that the other girl was not going to step in with her.

She still felt hot at the thought of that conversation. She should have denied it all; she should have left the office before they'd even got to that stage; she should have laughed off the suggestion. She should have, should have, should have. But she hadn't.

Helen Scott was basically an unpleasant person; Francesca had always known that from the very first moment that she had set eyes on her. She shuddered at the thought that that sly, curling mouth might start rumours snowballing through the building.

When she got into her flat the telephone was ringing, and Francesca picked up the receiver, balancing it under her chin while she tried to wriggle out of her coat. It was Oliver.

'I'll be delayed by a bit more than a week,' he said, with his usual lack of preliminaries. His voice sounded distant and hollow, and there was a slight crackle down the line. 'Things are moving slightly slower here than I had imagined.' There was a sigh, and she could imagine him rubbing his eyes with his thumbs.

'No problem,' she said brightly, feeling utterly dejected at this piece of news. 'I'm doing fine at work. I've been in touch with Ben Johnson about that contract and I shall fax him the information he wants tomorrow first thing.' She thought of Helen and wondered what he would say if she told him that on another front things weren't humming along nicely at all.

'Good,' he said in a clipped voice. 'And how are you?'

'Nice of you to ask,' she replied, suddenly happy. 'I'm fine.'

'So you're fine and work is fine.' There was a touch of harshness in his voice and she speculated on what that meant. Was he missing her? Had he hoped that she wouldn't be fine, that she would be missing him? She couldn't hear him very well, though, and long-distance lines distorted voices, but if her imagination was playing tricks on her then her imagination was also doing a good job of improving her mood.

Not that she was about to tell him how she was really feeling. She knew that he wanted to be casual about their relationship, and she intended to be as casual about it as he was. If he got the slightest idea that she was playing a game of deadly seriousness, then he would turn his back on her faster than the speed of light.

'Shall I postpone all those meetings that were lined up for you on your return?' she asked, still in her cheerful voice.

'Of course,' he said briefly. 'I can hardly be in two places at once, can I?'

They chatted about work for a while longer, and when he rang off she was feeling distinctly happier than she had been an hour previously.

On the spur of the moment she decided to give Rupert a call, and after a few sheepish apologies from him about not being in touch recently she talked him into coming over.

'You can share dinner with me,' she said temptingly. 'Corned beef sandwiches.'

'Irresistible.' He laughed. 'I'm on my way.'

Actually—and she told herself that that had not been the point of the phone call—she wanted to ask him about Imogen.

And he had expected that. She could tell from the expression on his face the minute he walked through the door. It was a mixture of guilt and wariness, and as soon as he had been settled with a glass of wine—the only alcohol in the place—he said, obviously taking the bull by the horns, 'I meant to tell you, I'm going out with someone you know. Imogen Sattler.' There was hearty bluster in his voice, but his face was red.

'Really?' Francesca said, raising her eyebrows expressively, and he battled on, not drinking, his hands cradling the glass.

'I would have told you sooner, but you know how it is...' His voice fizzled out and she smiled.

'Naughty, naughty Rupert. Imogen Sattler was spoken for.'

'The engagement is off.'

Francesca looked at him, frowning, thinking. Earlier, speaking to Oliver on the phone, she had pushed aside any uncomfortable thoughts about what had happened between him and Imogen. Now she found herself wondering. She found herself thinking of Helen. 'Did he decide that you would do; you would tide him through a bad night?'

'Neither of us meant anything to happen, Frankie.' The bluster had given way to earnestness, and he leaned forward. 'I thought she was fun, not like the other girls I've met in the past.' He frowned, and tried to be more descriptive than that. 'When I first saw her I didn't think she was that attractive. I mean, I thought she was a very nice-looking girl, but…'

'But not along the lines of Linda Baker,' Francesca filled in wryly, and he gave her a dry look in return. Linda Baker had been one of his past girlfriends—an impeccably beautiful girl with an impeccable background and not much happening between her two ears. If the rooms in Imogen's head were all filled and busy, there had been quite a few in Linda's which hadn't been opened up for a while—if ever.

'But not along the lines of Linda Baker,' he agreed. 'I also thought that she was humouring me when she told me how much she enjoyed the nightclub—you know, the time I dragged her and that boss of yours along.'

Francesca nodded. 'And things just went on from there, Rupert?'

'She phoned me up. We chatted. I telephoned her. I happened to be passing right outside her office one day and we went out for a drink. It was all above board, honestly.'

'You don't have to convince me of anything, Rupert,' she said mildly. 'I'm not here to sit in judgement on you.'

'I feel badly about Oliver Kemp, though,' he muttered, and she knew that he would. It was not in his nature to steal other men's girlfriends, but theft, in that instance, would have been a two-way affair, wouldn't it?

'We just had so much to talk about,' he clarified helplessly. 'She was different. She had more intelligence in one little finger than all the other girls I'd ever been out with combined. I couldn't understand what she saw in a lump like me. I don't suppose I ever will.'

There was such genuine wonder in his voice that Francesca had to smile. It would not occur to him that what he had was unique—his good nature, his thoughtfulness, his happy, carefree disposition. It was a different kind of appeal from the overt aggressive masculinity that Oliver had, but she thought, it carried its own weight.

'I began to think about her all the time,' he carried on. 'I stopped going out. I felt that I needed to be by the phone in case she called. We weren't sleeping together,' he felt compelled to add, 'but we both knew that it would happen, and we both knew that she had to break off the engagement.

'She told me that she and Oliver had been friends for years, but that the engagement had been a mistake. Friendship had never matured into love. At least not for her. She had thought at the time that it would be enough, but then she met me...' He couldn't prevent a small, satisfied smile from forming.

'So there you have it. As it turned out, Oliver called the whole thing off anyway. Told her that she deserved to pursue what she wanted.' He sipped some of the wine and sat back with his fingers entwined on his lap. 'Any questions?'

He sounded like a professor addressing his students, and Francesca shook her head. No questions. None that concerned him, anyway.

She listened while Rupert spent the next couple of hours chatting, mostly about Imogen, but things were going around in her head, and as soon as he left she began thoughtfully tidying the room.

Oliver had broken the engagement, true enough, but from where she was standing, with the jigsaw pieces neatly slotted together, it seemed very much like an act of generosity propelled by circumstance. His lover had wanted to be free and he had given her her freedom before she could demand it.

'Did he decide that you would do?'

A man on the rebound could be very undiscriminating, couldn't he? Was that why Oliver had come to see her? The woman he loved had told him that she was not in love with him, was going out with someone else, in fact, and he knew where he could find a willing woman with whom he could drown his sorrows? He hadn't looked like a man with a broken heart when he had come round, but then, thinking about it, Oliver Kemp was not the sort of man to walk around with a long face, was he?

No wonder he had told her that he wasn't interested in commitment. He was committed somewhere else—that was the reason.

On the rebound, she thought to herself. I had flung myself at him once, and he had walked away because his heart was somewhere else. He knew where to come; he knew that I would not turn him away. He didn't know why, but that didn't matter.

What mattered was that she would now have to face the truth. Oliver Kemp wanted a body—temporarily—and she was no longer happy to be a yielding one just because she had optimistically believed that time would make love grow. The soil there was barren. Nothing would grow.

Oliver Kemp loved Imogen, with her intellect, her gritty rise from rags to riches. He probably loved her more now that she was out of reach and for ever would be.

He could never love me, Francesca thought, with my cosseted upbringing and an intellect that has never had to strive to attain anything.

Now she was glad that he wasn't going to be back on schedule—glad that she had been given time to compose herself and do what she knew she had to do.

CHAPTER SIX

'YOU look sick,' Helen said with a sort of nasty satisfaction. They were in the cloakroom and Francesca was staring at her reflection in the mirror and wondering whether a dab of lipstick might improve her green complexion.

'I feel fine,' she muttered, lying. She felt awful. In fact, she had been feeling awful for the past fortnight, thinking about Oliver and that resignation letter which he would find on his desk when he returned the following morning.

'Could have fooled me.' Helen stood behind her so that their eyes met in the mirror. 'Claire Burns said that you looked like death warmed up when she came to see you the other morning.'

Claire Burns, thought Francesca, wouldn't have been snide with it.

'You should be feeling on top of the world, what with your lover coming back tomorrow.'

Francesca couldn't help a furtive look around to make sure that the cloakroom was empty, even though she knew that it was, and Helen laughed slyly.

'The coast is clear,' she said, sneering. 'Just the two of us and our little secret.' Which only made Francesca feel sick all over again, and she rushed into the toilet, only just managing to slam the door behind her.

When she emerged Helen had gone, and she slowly made her way back to her office. Her resignation letter was sitting in the top drawer of her desk like an unexploded bomb, and it had been there ever since Rupert had visited her at the flat, ever since her mind had been made up for her, and she had been drained of all reason for living. Or so it seemed.

It was just as well that she had never let him suspect her feelings for him, and just as well that she had kept their telephone conversation for the past weeks on a cheerful, impersonal note, never once betraying how much she yearned for those few minutes every day when she would hear his distant voice down the line.

In fact, since she had made up her mind to resign she had made sure that her voice was downright cool. That way she could prepare herself for the inevitable.

Nevertheless, Francesca was highly nervous the following morning when she arrived at work. She had left her unexploded bomb on his desk, so that he could read it and digest it without her standing in front of him like a tense schoolgirl.

She still had to face her father about her decision, and the quicker she left, the quicker her life could carry on.

I'll get over him in no time at all, she told herself, hanging her coat on the peg and walking across to her desk. She hadn't quite made it there when the connecting door opened, and she half turned, feeling a sick feeling in the pit of her stomach when she saw Oliver standing there, looming in the doorway, his eyes cold.

The impact of seeing him again after more than four weeks only made her realise how devastatingly handsome he was. She had forgotten how tall and overpowering his physical presence was, though she hadn't forgotten the sort of effect he had on her. He was having that effect now. She looked at him and felt that rush of awareness, that excited sensitivity to every last little detail of his appearance.

She also had a sudden, very sharp and very unwelcome

memory of the last time they'd seen each other, naked and in bed after the most wonderful night she had ever had in her entire life—a night when foolish optimism had been born and cold reality had been conveniently shoved into the background.

Foolish optimism, she thought, was hardly a worthwhile emotion, but she would certainly have preferred it to the lurch of dread that washed over her now, making her feel dizzy.

'Come into my office.' His face was unsmiling when he said that, and before she could say anything he had turned his back and vanished.

Francesca took three deep breaths to steady herself and followed him, quietly closing the door behind her. Then she sat down on the chair facing him and folded her arms on her lap.

'Did everything go all right on your trip?' she asked when the silence had stretched so taut that she could feel nervous perspiration breaking out all over her.

He was sitting staring at her, his eyes hard, his elbows resting on his desk. 'What does this mean?' He ignored her pleasantry, which she had known he would, and picked up the letter between two fingers as though it were contagious.

'Oh,' Francesca replied, her mind going blank, 'so you've read it.'

'No,' he answered, his deep voice thick with sarcasm. 'I've called you in here so that I could play a guessing game with you. Of course I've damn well read it.' He stood up so abruptly that she jumped, and then he stalked across to the window; he perched on the ledge and looked at her, his arms folded.

She had rehearsed this little scene quite a number of times in her head, but now, reluctantly staring up at his menacing figure, she realised that no amount of dress re-hearsals had prepared her for this.

'Might I ask why you've decided to resign?' he asked coldly, and she licked her lips.

'Ah.' She frowned and struggled to remember her little speech. 'I've decided that this isn't the sort of job that I'm looking for,' she said, which bore no resemblance at all to her rehearsed speech.

'Too uninteresting?' His mouth curled.

'No. It's very stimulating,' she responded quickly, truth-fully.

'Not well paid enough?'

'No, of course not! I have no idea where I could get a job with a bigger salary.'

'So why are you leaving a stimulating job with an in-comparable pay cheque?'

Good question, she thought miserably, trying to come up with an equally good answer. 'It's just not what I'm looking for...' was all she could find to say, and his brows snapped together in an angry frown.

'Oh, let's stop playing games, Francesca, shall we? Why don't you admit that the reason you're leaving is because we slept together.'

There was a heavy silence, and the colour crept into her face.

'That has nothing to do with it,' she muttered, and he banged his fist on the table.

'Stop it!'

'All right, then!' she snapped, her head flying up. 'I admit it. I'm leaving because we slept together.'

'Well, at least we're getting somewhere now.' He sat back down at his desk. 'What difference does it make to your job whether we went to bed together or not?'

'I can't work with you and...'

'Oh, grow up, Francesca,' he said impatiently. 'Do you think that I'm going to make passes at you the minute you set foot inside the office?'

'No!' This was another one of those verbal traps, she thought. He was very good at that. He should have been a lawyer.

'Then...?' He gave her a cool, stripping look, and she had to force herself not to launch into a mumbling, incoherent explanation.

'It's just that I've decided that I'm not attracted to you. When I first came here you told me in no uncertain terms that I wasn't your type, and I guess you're not my type either.' She was sure that he would see through that; she was sure that anyone would see through a lie that was as big as a house, but his expression didn't change, and when he replied the temperature in his voice had dropped by a couple of degrees.

'I see,' he said with glacial politeness. 'I still can't see what that has to do with your resigning. Have you now decided that I'm so repulsive that you can't bear to be anywhere near me?'

There was deep distaste in his voice when he said that and she wondered whether he was thinking that she was nothing more than a rich young thing, utterly immature, who had thrown herself at his feet only to retreat hurriedly once the plunge had been taken. In the real world, she knew, they would shrug and carry on, with life settling back into its normal routine, and their one night together relegated to history.

She couldn't begin to know how to answer his question, and he stared at her, waiting, for such a long time that she eventually dropped her eyes and gave a small shrug.

'Look,' he said, and his voice was that of someone older and wiser addressing a recalcitrant child. 'You're a good secretary, and it's taken me a hell of a long time finding one. Believe it or not, I'm not going to take advantage of you. We slept together once, but don't think that I see that as some kind of perk to which I'm now automatically entitled.'

He leaned forward. 'Francesca, why don't you open your eyes and wake up to the real world? Men and women sleep together for all sorts of reasons, and they make mistakes. Life carries on, though.'

'I know that.' So she was a mistake. He couldn't have cut her deeper if he had pulled out a ten-inch carving-knife and run it through her heart. The pain was so intense that she had to take a deep, shaky breath to keep from collapsing.

'You'll have to find me a replacement,' he continued, and she knew that she should be overjoyed that the situation had been resolved, but she had to bite back the tears. So this was how that subtle game of sexual courtship was played. In a game without love, indifference made retreat so easy.

'Of course.' She nodded, struggling to think of a suitable platitude that might restore her self-control, and discovering that platitudes were never around when you needed them. 'Have you got any specifications?'

'Someone,' he said in a hard voice, 'who is prepared to view the job as a long-term proposition.'

'I'm sorry...' she began, faltering, and he cut in harshly. 'Forget it. If I'd known that you'd react to what happened between us in such a hysterical way, I wouldn't have come near you.'

'But you couldn't resist, could you?' Bitterness restored some of her spirit, and she looked at him without flinching.

His eyes narrowed. 'What the heck are you talking about now?'

'Imogen ended your relationship and you just couldn't resist sleeping with me as an afterthought, because you knew that I would be willing.'

'So that's what this is all about.' He leaned back in his chair, looking as sympathetic as a cobra about to strike. 'You're quitting because of a case of severe pique.'

If he had intended to make her feel ten years old, he couldn't have succeeded more. She flushed and looked away, and he laughed under his breath. It wasn't a pleasant sound.

'No one likes to be used,' she muttered.

'You seem to enjoy every minute of it,' he drawled. 'Or did I misread the situation?'

'I was a fool.' If I was your mistake, she thought, then you can be mine—or at least that's what I shall let you believe.

'What were you hoping for after one night together, Francesca? Love and marriage?'

That was so near the mark that she had to fight not to betray her emotions. 'No. But I didn't think at the time that I was a fill-in for someone else—someone who was no longer available.'

'I'm not some kind of sex-crazed animal,' he said coolly. 'I wanted you and the feeling was mutual. We slept together. End of equation.'

'And now you think that we can continue working happily together as though nothing had happened?'

'Nothing *has* happened,' he said. 'But this is a pointless argument. I'm not going to persuade you to stay; you've already made your mind up and I have no intention of beating my head against a brick wall. There's some correspondence still to be finished. Once you've done that, and, of course, found someone to replace you, you can leave.'

'Thank you,' she said, wondering what she was thanking him for exactly. For ruining her life? For treating her as a disposable object of desire? She knew that she could hardly blame him for that, not when she had so readily made herself available, no questions asked, no answers expected, but she did anyway.

She stood up and let herself out, and immediately went to the cloakroom, where she had to fight down the desire to be sick. Again.

When she got back to her desk he had gone, and there was a note with some instructions, and three letters to be typed.

She ignored all of them. She telephoned the employment agency instead and lined up four interviews for the afternoon. Keep busy, she thought. Time enough to make misery your companion.

It was with some uncertain relief that she found two of them proved very promising. One was a woman in her mid-thirties, who was returning to work after some years of rearing children, and the other was a middle-aged woman who had moved down from the north with her husband, who had had a company transfer. They both looked capable and easy to work with.

As soon as Oliver returned at five-thirty that afternoon she told him.

'Hire whichever seemed better,' he told her, making his way past her desk into his office, and she spun around, astonished.

'But don't you want to see them for yourself?'

He stopped at the door and looked back at her. 'Trust your instinct,' he said, with a cold smile. 'It may have let you down in one department, but I'm sure it's working well enough in others.' And he closed the door behind him.

So she telephoned the agency, told them which of the

two she had decided to take on, arranged a starting day, contacted the personnel department, and then remained working for another hour, busily doing as much as she could because she now had the impression that Oliver wanted her out sooner rather than later. He had tried to keep her on, and, having failed in that, had washed his hands of her and her infantile scruples.

Well, that suits me fine, she thought to herself, banging away on the keyboard and wishing that it was Oliver Kemp's head.

He left shortly before she did, nodding briefly in her direction, and when she next glanced at her watch it was after six-thirty and she was feeling light-headed and ill with hunger.

She stopped off at the supermarket—or rather at what optimistically called itself a supermarket when in fact it was little more than a corner shop with a stock supply of the most basic tinned food, and a selection of vegetables that always looked as though they had seen happier days.

It was only later that night, after she had consumed a large, hastily prepared meal and was lying in bed, that her wayward thoughts began to take a different direction. By the time she fell asleep she knew that she would have to leave the company the following day if possible.

Francesca arrived at work late the next morning—the first time since she had started—and immediately went into Oliver's office, after knocking and pushing open the door.

He was on the telephone and he pointed to the chair facing him, carrying on his conversation, his voice clipped and authoritative. She watched him surreptitiously, imprinting on her mind for ever the taut lines of his body, the curve of his mouth, the wintry grey-blue of his eyes. And she wondered.

'Yes,' he said to her as soon as he had replaced the receiver.

'I've found a replacement,' she told him without preamble. 'A youngish woman with two small children. She's been out of the workforce for a few years, but I gave her an impromptu typing test and she sailed through it. She's worked in this sort of field before, though it was a long time ago, but she's bright and enthusiastic and I think she'll catch on without too much difficulty.'

'What's her name?'

'Jessica Hines. She'll start tomorrow.' Francesca paused and looked at him in the eye. 'I've brought everything up to date, and I thought that if I spent the rest of the week showing her the ropes I might make Friday my last day.'

He shrugged and said, 'Sure.'

She stood up, ready to leave, but before she could turn the handle of the door he was standing next to her. He leaned against the door, looking down at her. When she breathed, she breathed him in—that masculine aroma that was as powerful to her senses as incense.

'I'm not around for much of the week,' he said in a low voice, 'so I want to say something to you before you go now, in case the opportunity doesn't arise again.'

'What is it?'

'Look at me,' he commanded, and she steeled herself to do it, to raise her eyes to his.

'I don't want you to leave here thinking that the only reason I made love to you that night was because I was suffering from a broken heart and I needed a bit of female companionship.'

'There's no need to explain anything to me,' Francesca retorted, with a spark of bitter anger in her voice.

'Yes, there is. Emotionally you haven't grown up, and

this is the sort of thing that you could dwell on until it assumed proportions way beyond control.'

'Thank you for being so thoughtful,' she said sarcastically, wincing at the unintended insult. The fact that he had not meant to offend her by describing her as a child at the beck and call of her emotions only made the offence worse.

'What we did that night was totally spontaneous. When I touched you I wasn't touching Imogen in some maudlin, nostalgic way.'

'You loved her, though.'

'Is that a question or a statement of fact?'

'An observation.'

He didn't answer that. Instead he said, angling his head away from her, 'I would rather you didn't leave.' There was a dark flush on his neck and a certain harshness in his voice that made her realise that he was uncomfortable. Was this the first time that he had ever asked anyone to do something; the first time that he had not told, knowing that he would be obeyed?

He had risen through life the hard way, had never had doors opened for him. He had had to open them all himself, and in the process he had become accustomed to forging forward, to taking steps that needed to be taken in order to gain what could be gained.

She felt a powerful, searing pang of sheer wanting—wanting to listen to him, to stay in a job she enjoyed, to feed her addiction to him. But, of course, all that was impossible. Youthful optimism had been shed for ever, and now she couldn't even really remember how she could have nurtured any wild hopes that he would one day love her if she persevered hard enough.

'I can't stay,' she said flatly, and he pulled back, shoving his hands in his pockets.

'Fine. In that case I won't keep you further.' He walked back to his desk and sat down. 'You have a list of my meetings for the rest of the week,' he said briefly, not looking at her but flicking through a file on the desk and extracting bits of paper from it. 'I shall be out for most of the day, but if you need to talk to me I'll be accessible on my mobile phone or at the client. You can arrange for me to have lunch with Mrs Hines tomorrow. I should be able to manage that.'

'Of course.'

'Good. You can go now.'

He hadn't looked at her once, even though she stupidly knew that she was hovering a bit by the door.

'That's all, Francesca,' he said, looking up, and she nodded and left his office.

Well, she thought, sitting down in front of her computer terminal, that's that. Life goes on. Time heals. There were countless clichés she could think of and none of them gave her a scrap of comfort. What she saw ahead of her wasn't life carrying on, or time healing. It was a dark tunnel— because everything had changed, and it was as if she had now found herself in a strange new world where she no longer knew the rules. What was going to happen now?

She didn't want to think about it. Not now. Not yet. There would be time enough for that.

Not for the first time she desperately wished that her mother was still alive. She could share most things with her father, but what she was going through now needed a woman's wisdom. She could understand for the first time why her father had felt compelled to try and make up for her mother's absence from her life, why he had felt guilty that although he could give her a lot it would never be enough.

*   *   *

The following day Jessica came, bright and keen and like a breath of fresh air.

Oliver had her in his office briefly, but he was virtually on his way out. It was enough time, though, to leave quite an impression on Jessica, who emerged, sat next to Francesca at the desk, and said in a slightly shell-shocked voice, 'He's awfully overpowering, isn't he?'

'You'll get used to it,' Francesca replied, reaching for the top file on the desk and spreading it open between them. She didn't want to talk about Oliver Kemp.

'Did you?'

'Yes,' she said tonelessly. She wondered whether she really would have if she had needed the job and the money as desperately as Jessica needed it. Her husband was a painter and decorator—a job which depended largely on all sorts of things beyond his control—and he was finding work thin on the ground at the moment. The money that Jessica earned would be vital to their standard of living.

'He may work you hard,' Francesca said, brightening up her voice—after all, there was no point in spreading doubts and tarnishing the other girl's enthusiasm—'but he's very fair and he's very patient at explaining things.' Bit of an exaggeration, that last one, but she said it anyway, and it seemed to have the desired effect of relieving some of Jessica's anxiety.

They worked non-stop for the remainder of the day, apart from the break when Oliver took Jessica to lunch, and by the time Friday rolled around enough had been explained so that Francesca could make her departure without thinking that she had left someone floundering in the deep blue sea.

At five-thirty she found herself taking her time with her coat, taking her time looking around the office for the last time, hoping that Oliver would stride in so that she could have one last look at him before he vanished out of her life for ever. But there was no sign of him.

She had hardly seen him at all that week. Meetings had kept him out of the office most of the time, and when he had been around he had liaised with Jessica, with Francesca only a background presence, there to clarify bits and pieces.

She was leaving the building, hurrying in the direction of the Underground, when Helen appeared from no-where—materialised, Francesca thought with an inward groan of despair, like a vampire.

'How are you?' Helen asked, falling into step with her.

'Fine,' Francesca said tightly. It wasn't anywhere near the truth, because she had never felt worse in her life, but the question was not one that required a truthful answer. As with most things that Helen said to her it was a prelude to something altogether nastier.

'Sure? I don't believe you!'

'That's fine by me.'

They had arrived at the station and they both joined the queue for tickets. On a Friday night, at rush hour, the place was packed, and the crowds, the harsh fluorescent lighting, Helen's presence there at her elbow all combined to make Francesca feel giddy and sick. She could feel Helen's sharp little eyes on her, watching the sudden pallor of her skin.

'I hear that you're leaving,' she said conversationally, and Francesca didn't say anything. 'What brought about that sudden decision?'

Francesca wished that the queue would move a bit faster. There were at least fifteen people ahead of her, and naturally the man at the counter, as luck would have it, was taking an inordinately long time because he couldn't find his wallet.

'Still—wise, I suppose,' Helen said conversationally. 'I'd have done the same. He only slept with you because you were there at the right time in the right place.'

There was a thread of bitter envy in her voice. Helen must know, Francesca thought, that Oliver Kemp was simply not interested in her, was probably totally unaware of her existence, in fact, but that didn't stop her from taking a malicious delight in spoiling what she saw as a relationship she could have had.

'A girl's got to have her pride. What are you going to do now?'

'Get another job,' Francesca said shortly. The man had at last found his wallet, after what seemed like an all-out search through every nook and cranny of his overcoat, suit jacket and briefcase, and the line was moving swiftly forward. Thank God.

'But will you be able to?' Helen asked softly from behind her, and Francesca felt her body stiffen in alarm. What did that mean?

'There are lots of vacancies for secretaries,' she said, still feeling that dreadful flutter of alarm move around inside her.

She paid for her ticket, turned around, and said, in a final parting shot, 'I should forget Oliver Kemp if I were you. He's not interested in you and he never will be. You're wasting your time.'

'So we're more alike than you care to think, then?' Helen said, but her eyes were hard stones. 'Still, best of luck with what you move on to do.' She smiled that feline smile. 'And I know you'll be pleased to hear that your leaving has made way for me.'

'What are you talking about now?'

'Oh, nothing really. Nothing that affects you now, anyway. Just that I saw Oliver today and I managed to persuade him to let me take over your job. After all, my typing may need a bit of home improvement, but I *do* know an awful lot about the company, and I *do* know an awful lot about the clients. Jessica is going to slot into my old department. He's going to tell her on Monday.' Sly eyes gleamed from under heavily mascaraed eyelashes. 'Wasn't it sweet of him to give me a go?'

Francesca didn't say a word. She turned her back and almost ran to her platform. She felt hot, sick and desperate to get back to her flat.

Employing Helen Scott behind her back seemed the ultimate betrayal. Would *she* end up in his bed as well? Francesca wondered feverishly.

She spent the next week hibernating, too lethargic to do anything and with too many thoughts on her mind. They weighed her down, made her sluggish and tearful.

She didn't want to think about Oliver, but she did. She didn't want to think about Helen Scott, but she did. And then there were all those other equally consuming worries—like how she was going to cope and how she could tell her father. An uneasy silence now lay between them—her doing, she knew, but uneasy silences were the hardest to break, and this news was the worst possible way of breaking this one.

She was sitting with a cup of tea on Friday night, with the television switched on, half following a complicated plot which seemed to involve a lot of running around and a lot of baffled faces of detectives trying to solve a string of murders but mostly thinking, when there was a sharp knock on the door.

She took a deep breath, frowning at the intrusion, opened the door and stood still in shock.

'What are you doing here?' she whispered, with panic in her voice.

Oliver's pale eyes were cold, but his mouth smiled, and he said lightly, 'Is that any way to greet your ex-boss?'

Francesca made no move to pull open the door. 'Why have you come?'

'To find out how you are, of course,' he said in the same light voice, while his eyes remained cool and hard. He reached out and pushed back the door, and then walked into the room, leaving her two options—either to close the door behind her and muster up some kind of self-composure, or else to stand by the open door and yell at the top of her voice that she wanted him to leave.

She closed the door behind her and he prowled around the small room, pausing to look out of the window, which offered a particularly uninspiring view of the street below—not a tree within sight, no patch of green, but then this was London.

'Would you like a cup of coffee?' she asked awkwardly, and he nodded.

'If it's no bother.'

'No bother at all.' They sounded like two distant acquaintances who had unexpectedly found themselves thrown together in an artificial situation and were trying to make polite conversation.

She made a cup of coffee, handed it to him, then sat down on the chair, hitching her legs up, and contemplated him with as much detachment as she could muster. Wasn't facing a problem, she told herself, the first step to curing it?

'So how are you?' he asked, sipping some of his coffee and giving her the full blast of that off-putting stare of his.

She said a little defensively, 'I'm fine.'

'Told your father that you've left?' he asked, still casually, and she shook her head.

'I haven't spoken to him since... Well, I'll do that next week,' she murmured vaguely.

'Difficult breaking bad news, isn't it?' He gave her a cold smile and stared at her, which made her feel uncomfortable and suddenly very resentful of his presence in her flat. She had not asked him to come. She had certainly not wanted to see him. All she wanted was to forget about him.

'Have you started looking for something else?' he asked, and she shook her head.

'I'll start next week,' she muttered.

He said with heavy sarcasm. 'Busy week ahead of you, wouldn't you say?'

'Yes,' she agreed. She felt oddly threatened by his tone, like someone who had suddenly spotted a shark in the swimming pool.

'There's a vacancy at the company,' he said, looking at her closely. 'Maria Barnes has left to work for her brother-in-law, and Gerald Fox, one of the financial directors, is looking for a replacement. The job is yours if you want it.'

'No!' She spoke quickly and loudly. Return to that company? It was utterly impossible. She couldn't have taken that job if she had been down to her last penny and had nothing else in the offing.

'No?' He shook his head, and she could tell from the expression on his face that her answer had not surprised him in the slightest. He had expected it.

She wished that he would go. She felt so nervous that her fingers were gripping the sides of the chair and the heavy beating of her heart was making her feel faint.

'Why did Maria decide to leave?' she asked, licking her lips and knowing that if she could keep the conversation on an impersonal level she might be able to get through it. 'I thought that she liked working there.'

'Oh, she did,' Oliver agreed, running his finger round the rim of the cup. 'But her brother-in-law's firm isn't doing too well, and he can't afford a full-time secretary even though he needs one. She's going to take a big cut in her salary, in return for which they're going to give her the top floor of their house so that she doesn't have to pay any rent.' He raised his eyes to hers, and there was hard irony there. 'Desperate situations sometimes need desperate solutions, don't they, Francesca?'

He stood up and placed the cup very gently down on the table in front of him. 'You look a little tired,' he said, moving across to her. 'Shall I leave you in peace now?'

She nodded, relieved, and he said, still very calmly, 'I won't come round again, if you'd rather I didn't.'

She nodded again, putting her feet to the ground to see him out, but he said immediately, 'Don't get up. Please.' He smiled, and there was definitely something very alarming about that smile now. He leaned forward, over her, resting his hands on either side of her chair.

'We wouldn't want you to tire yourself even more, would we, Francesca?'

'What do you mean?' she asked faintly.

'What do I mean? I'll tell you what I mean. Did you think that I wouldn't find out? You're pregnant, aren't you?'

CHAPTER SEVEN

IT TOOK a little while for that to register. For a few seconds Francesca's mind went completely blank, but then it started working again and her face whitened.

'Who told you?' There didn't seem any point playing games. For one thing the dark rage on his face, which she realised now had been lurking there all along, was frightening her, and for another he would be able to find out easily enough that she *was* pregnant. All he had to do was watch her, and as sure as day broke and night fell he would see her putting on weight.

When she had found out that she was pregnant her immediate thought had been that she had to resign, but her thought processes seemed to have ended there. Now they sensibly moved one step further, and she realised that there was a good chance that he would have found out anyway. He knew her father, and no doubt they would have arranged to meet again, and then it would all have come out.

She had not planned on telling her father the identity of the baby's father, but that would have been immaterial. Oliver would have worked it out for himself. It would only have taken some elementary mathematics.

She put her hand to her forehead, and he pulled it away and pinned it to the chair with his fingers.

'How did you find out?' she asked faintly, and he bared his teeth in a cold smile.

'Does it matter? Helen Scott, one of the girls who works in the company, mentioned that you had been looking sick

119

for the past couple of weeks and said that she thought you might be pregnant.'

That was a bitter pill. She closed her eyes and wondered when these little confidences had taken place and where. At his desk, with her sitting provocatively on the edge? Over a drink in a bar somewhere? In bed?

She should have known that Helen would have suspected, and now that little cryptic comment at the station about finding another job—whether she would be able to—made a lot more sense than it had then.

At the time she had thought that the other girl had been making some guarded, spiteful remark based on an ill-founded suspicion that the reason she was leaving was because she couldn't handle the job, but she had been much closer to the mark than that, hadn't she? In fact, she had scored a bull's eye on the first shot.

'Why didn't you say what you wanted to say the minute you walked through the door?' Francesca asked resentfully. 'Why the charade?'

'I thought I'd give you time,' he said savagely. 'I thought I'd beat around the bush enough so that you would come right out and tell me, if that was what you intended doing, but you didn't.'

'Why should I?' Francesca asked tightly, looking up at him. 'It's not your concern.'

That, she realised, had been a poor choice of words. His face darkened, and she began to stammer incoherently. 'What I mean is…what I meant to say…'

'I know exactly what you meant to say, Francesca. But you'd better get it through that head of yours right now that it is my concern!'

'It's your baby,' she agreed heatedly, 'but that's about it. I don't want anything from you. In fact, I wish you'd just vanish out of my life. I wish you'd never come here in the first place!'

She really did too. He would never understand how he had ruined her life, because what she had given him was much more than a night of love-making, and she couldn't see how she would ever be able to recover from the wreckage and start piecing her life together again if he saw the baby as his concern, and decided that he was to be a permanent fixture on the scene.

If at the beginning she had not seen beyond handing in her resignation and optimistically thinking that he would never find out, her thought processes had now jumped ahead by several leagues, and she imagined a life ahead of her with him appearing in it regularly, so that he could keep in contact with his child—keep in contact even when another Imogen Sattler came along. How was she going to face that?

If Helen had wanted to deliver a final piece of misdirected spite, she could not have chosen a more effective way—to usurp her job and to disclose her pregnancy. He had allowed the first and now he would destroy her for the second.

'Well, I'm here now, lady, and if you think that you're going to get rid of me then you're mistaken.'

'But why...?' she asked in a raw voice. She rubbed her wrist where he had been holding it, and risked another quick glance at his face to see whether some of his anger had subsided. It hadn't.

'Why? You must think I'm a number-one bastard if you believe I can casually get a woman pregnant and then walk away from my responsibility as though it didn't exist.'

So this is what it feels like to be someone's responsibility, she thought. Not a very pleasant feeling. Almost as gut-wrenching as being someone's mistake.

He raked his fingers through his hair and went back to the sofa, sitting down heavily, leaning forward with his elbows on his knees and his hands lightly clasped together.

The funny thing about dreams, she thought, was that they rarely ever bore any resemblance to reality. She had always dreamed when she was young that life would pan out in a very normal manner for her—she would fall in love, she would get married, she would start a family, and every step of the way would be wondrously happy.

Yet here she was—in love all right, but with the wrong man, and starting a family all right, but in a loveless relationship. What a laugh. Except she wasn't remotely amused by any of it. She felt utterly miserable.

'You said that you were using contraception,' he said, breaking into her thoughts, and she looked across at him with an expression that was half defensiveness and half guilt.

'I lied,' she admitted, twisting her fingers together. 'I didn't think that anything would happen.' She saw his expression of impatient disbelief and rushed on, more in defence now than guilt, 'Well, it's not as though I sleep around! Why should I be using any contraception? On the off chance? Anyway, I didn't think that I would have the bad luck for this to happen on the one and only time I made love.'

'Well, it's happened, and now we've got to decide what we're going to do about it.'

'"Do about it"? "*Do* about it"? What does *that* mean? If you think that I'm going to get rid of it somehow, then you're wrong!'

'Don't be bloody stupid!' he bit out harshly. 'That's not what I'm saying at all.'

'Then what are you saying? It's too soon to start talking about visitation rights. Why don't we wait until it's born?'

He ignored that as if he wouldn't dignify the remark with a response. 'Like it or not, I'm the father of the child,' he said calmly, 'and there's only one thing for it—we're going to have to get married.'

'No!'

'Why not?'

'We don't love each other—' she began.

'Stop living in a dream world, Francesca,' he cut in harshly. 'This is reality, and the best thing we can do is get married. We can break it to your father in the morning.'

'We are not going to do any such thing!' Did he really think that she would agree to marry him, knowing that the only reason he was doing so was because of the baby? 'Shotgun marriages are always doomed to failure,' she informed him, and he laughed, but without much humour.

'And where do you get your statistics?'

'Everyone knows that,' she muttered stubbornly. 'I can manage perfectly well on my own. I don't need any financial help from you. I'll go back home and—'

'You will *not* go back home,' he said before she could finish. 'You will *not* use your father's money to bring up a child of mine.'

'Don't tell me what I can and can't do!'

They stared at each other silently, and after a while he said, getting up, 'I'm going to make myself a cup of coffee. Would you like one?'

'I've gone off it.'

'A glass of juice, then?'

She shrugged and nodded, and hoped that he would take his time, because she needed to get her thoughts into order.

He came back into the room eventually, handed her a glass of orange juice, and after a few minutes said conversationally, 'Feeling better now?'

She could see that even if she wasn't he most certainly was. There was no longer that violent anger on his face. He had regained that formidable self-composure and was looking at her over the rim of his cup, his eyes veiled.

'Shall we continue this conversation without any hysteria?' he asked, which made her bristle with resentment, but she didn't say anything and he carried on with calm confidence, 'I agree you don't need any financial help from me, but that doesn't begin to solve your problems. For instance, what do you think your father is going to say about your condition?'

'He won't be overjoyed, I know that,' Francesca muttered, looking down into her glass as if searching for inspiration. 'He'll be shocked and disappointed.'

Which, she thought, was putting it mildly. He had always tried so hard to do what was right for her, to compensate for the lack of maternal guidance.

Through all his long, hard, working hours he had always made time to come to her little school functions, to be there whenever it mattered. That was why he had been so worried when she had finished her secretarial course and had started going out with what he'd seen as entirely the wrong crowd. That was why her rift with him would now be causing him anxiety.

'He'll be even more shocked and disappointed when you tell him that you won't marry me even though I want you to,' Oliver murmured smoothly, and she glared at him.

'He'll understand.'

'Will he, though?'

'He'd rather I married for love than for all the wrong reasons.'

Oliver's lips thinned and he said silkily, 'Then I shall just have to convince him how much I love you, shan't I?' And now her eyes were helpless. 'There are worse things in life than marrying for the sake of a baby,' he said in a hard voice, but there was an angry need to persuade her there as well that made her frown. 'Two people can start out with stars in their eyes and the marriage can break down in a matter of weeks because there wasn't enough there to start with. At least we know each other.'

'In a manner of speaking.' Francesca put in with a certain amount of bitter sarcasm. 'Besides,' she continued, thinking about it, 'Dad would see through my phoney baloney about love in a minute flat.'

'No, he wouldn't. People are very good at believing what they want to believe, and, face it, I'm not exactly the human equivalent of the bubonic plague, am I?'

'Oh, very modest,' she snapped, and he laughed, and this time there was a great deal more humour there.

Although she would never admit it, he was right; they did know one another, perhaps better than she cared to say. Or at least *she* knew *him*. Wasn't that why she had fallen in love with him? She had seen the warm charm, the wit, the sense of fair play which were all there underneath the aggressive, terse exterior.

He'd implied that *he* knew *her*, though. But did he? He had thought her a child—a spoiled child who had sailed through life on the wings of money.

And she knew that he had not been initially attracted to her at all. She had not been his type. Maybe physically he had revised his opinions, for reasons which she did not know for certain but could make an educated guess at, but she still wasn't his type. If it hadn't been for the baby, he would never have dreamt of asking her to marry him. He might have continued sleeping with her, but it would have only been a temporary arrangement.

'Your father would prefer to know that you were being taken care of, rather than think of you as a single parent, emotionally struggling on her own to bring up a baby. You're still a child yourself, for God's sake.'

'There you go again! Thank you very much,' Francesca muttered.

'Think about it.' He put his cup on the table and stood up. 'I'll pay you a visit tomorrow morning.'

After he had gone she sank back onto her chair and stared sightlessly in front of her, thinking about what he had said.

She didn't think of herself as a child, but she could understand what Oliver meant. She had behaved impulsively with him, and with foolish naïvety had found herself in a situation that was going to catapult her into maturity whether she liked it or not.

It would worry her father knowing that she would be bringing a baby into the world without the security of a family unit. She had been born into a great deal of love, and if she had been the daughter of a single-parent family herself then it hadn't been his choice.

She also worried about how her father would cope with having a newborn baby in the house. He wasn't an old man, but sleepless nights could tire the most vigorous individual and he would feel obliged, she knew, to do his fair share—not out of duty but out of love.

When Oliver knocked on the door the following morning at eight o'clock Francesca looked as tired as she felt.

'Have you had any sleep?' he asked immediately, and she stepped back to let him in.

'Not much,' she admitted. 'Did you expect me to, after our conversation last night? I've been thinking about it, wondering what to do.'

'Have you had any breakfast?' he asked, changing the subject, and she shook her head.

'So in other words you're behaving in exactly the sensible manner any doctor would heartily recommend. No sleep, no food.'

It was Saturday so he wasn't dressed for work. He was wearing a pair of jeans and a cream shirt, and she hurriedly looked away so that he wouldn't see the pull of attraction on her face.

'Come on,' he said, chivvying her along, she thought sullenly, like a recalcitrant child. Had he treated Imogen like that? she wondered. No chance.

'Let me get you something to eat.' He settled her into the chair and she obediently remained there because she was feeling rather faint and sick—as she had been for what seemed to be an eternity. Presently she heard the sound of pans and cutlery, and he emerged after a while with a plate of scrambled egg and toast. Then he sat down and watched while she ate the lot. Making sure, she thought, that she didn't tip it all into the plant next to the chair, no doubt.

'Thank you,' she said when she had finished. 'That was very nice.' She walked into the kitchen and looked round her in disbelief.

'How many pans did you use to concoct this?' she asked incredulously.

'I mentioned I could cook,' he murmured, closer to her than she'd expected. 'I never said anything about being a tidy cook.' He took the plate from her and began washing up in a fairly slapdash manner, stacking the crockery onto the draining-board in an inelegant heap, so that she had to grab a teacloth and hurriedly dry it to prevent breakage.

'Now,' he said when they had finished, 'get dressed and let's go and pay your father a little visit.'

'He'll be out.'

'No, he won't. I telephoned him to tell him that we were

coming over. He's been worried, waiting for you to get in touch. He was delighted.'

'What?' She stared at him, aghast. 'How could you?'

'You have to tell him sooner or later about the pregnancy,' he replied evenly in that voice of his which she had come to recognise from working with him—the voice that implied that arguments were useless.

'Of course, and I intend to! I just don't need pushing.'

'You do,' he said mildly. 'You needed pushing to get a job and you need pushing to do this, or else you'll put it off until it overshadows every waking moment. You stormed out on your father over a piece of nonsense and you can't face the thought of returning with this revelation. That's how family feuds develop.'

Francesca ground her teeth together. The fact that he had a point only made her angrier.

Why had her life suddenly become so complicated? She might not have spent her time in the past single-mindedly heading towards a goal; she might have been somewhat ingenuous in her outlook that dilemmas were things that happened to other people, and that she could merrily trundle through life without too many worries to disturb the flat surface, but why had things now gone so completely awry?

She would dearly have liked to blame him, but that was impossible, and she was not enough of a believer in fate to blame that either.

Perhaps her father's enormous wealth had insulated her even more than she could ever have imagined. She had never had to face any hard knocks in her life and now she found herself in a situation with which she could scarcely cope.

Still, that didn't mean that Oliver Kemp was entitled to push her around, did it?

'I might as well tell you that I haven't made any decisions about…about what we talked about. Or rather what *you* talked about,' she said once they were inside his car and heading towards her father's house. 'So I have no idea why you want to come along with me to see Dad.'

He averted his attention from the road briefly to glance at her, and there was an unyielding expression on his face.

'I don't trust you to tell him,' he said bluntly.

'Stop interfering in my life!'

'You opened the door, Francesca,' he told her.

'Are you trying to tell me that this is all my fault?' she asked, on the verge of tears. 'Oh, isn't that typical of a man?'

'Stop being a fool,' he said, shoving his handkerchief across to her, and she blew her nose noisily into it.

'I'd feel happier explaining things if you weren't hovering there in the background. This is a very personal thing.'

'And one that concerns us both,' he reminded her grimly.

He swung his car through the gates that led up to the courtyard outside the house and then waited for her, his hands in his pockets, the stiff, cold wind blowing his black hair across his face, giving him a dark, rakish look.

Her father was waiting for them in the sitting room. Bridie bustled them through, casting suspicious glances in Oliver's direction whenever she thought herself unnoticed, wondering what this stranger was doing in the house.

'Hello, darling,' her father said hesitantly. 'I'm so very glad you're here.' He came across, and Francesca smiled automatically, but she felt dreadfully nervous inside. She had had enough time to steel herself for the inevitability of this, but now that the time had actually arrived she felt as desperately anxious as someone standing on a platform about to address hundreds of people only to find that she'd lost her notes.

'Oliver,' her father said, shaking his hand, 'what's this all about? Sit down the both of you.' He gestured vaguely to the sofa and Oliver sat down, patting the spot next to him, which made her father's eyebrows shoot up in surprise. 'Would you like some tea? Coffee?'

He didn't wait for an answer. He went across to the door, shouted for Bridie, who obviously was close at hand because she appeared within seconds, and asked her to fetch some coffee, 'and a few croissants.'

'Dad...' Francesca said in a faltering voice. 'I'm sorry about...about what happened. I accused you of things and...and I apologise.'

'It's already forgotten,' he said briskly, but there was a sheen in his eyes. 'Now,' he continued, once they were sorted out with something to eat and drink, 'whatever is this all about? I hope you haven't come to tell me that Francesca isn't up to the job, Oliver.' It was as if, she thought, that uncomfortable silence between them had never existed. If only everything could be resolved as painlessly as that.

'I think,' Oliver said calmly, 'that Francesca would like to break the news to you herself.'

He sat there, she thought, sipping his coffee, not looking in the slightest bit nervous. Was he made of steel? she wondered resentfully.

'News? What news?' her father asked a little more sharply, turning to her, and Francesca tried a soothing smile.

'Nothing to get excited about, Dad,' she said. 'It's just...quite simply...that...' Oh, God, she thought, taking refuge in her coffee which tasted quite revolting to her.

She could feel their eyes on her and her stomach gave a lurch. 'What I'm trying to say here, Dad, is that...'

She looked helplessly at Oliver, who said calmly, 'Francesca has resigned.'

'What?'

'Dad!' She could feel herself in deep water now, without a lifebelt in sight. 'I... Yes, I've resigned.'

'Why?'

'Ah. Why?' she said, pointlessly playing for time. 'I don't quite know how I'm going to tell you this,' she continued, in the manner of someone looking for divine inspiration and not finding it, 'and I know that you're going to be shocked and disappointed...' at this point, she didn't dare meet her father's eyes, because the last thing she wanted to see was his shock and disappointment '...but I've been rather silly...'

'Not from my point of view,' Oliver murmured from next to her, and she felt the brush of his arm as he extended it along the back of the sofa behind her.

Her father wasn't looking too shocked or disappointed at this juncture. He just looked bewildered.

'Dad,' she blurted out, 'I'm pregnant.'

There was a deathly silence, and when she sneaked a glance at her father she saw that his mouth was half-open. It would have been comical in any other situation.

'And before you collapse on the spot,' Oliver said smoothly, taking it all in his stride, as though breaking news like this was a daily occurrence, 'we're going to get married.' He bent across to kiss the side of her face, and she went scarlet.

'I haven't—' she began.

He cut in swiftly. 'No, we haven't set a date yet, but it'll be sooner rather than later. Won't it, darling?' he said, and she could feel from the warmth of his breath on her face that he had turned to her.

Her father had still not come up for air, but eventually he said, 'Frankie? Pregnant? Getting married? What has been going on here?'

She began to splutter out that yes, she was pregnant, but that no, marriage was not on the cards, but she hardly had time to formulate a coherent sentence when Oliver said, still in that controlled, unfazed tone of voice, 'We're both a little surprised at how things have turned out, but we're also delighted, aren't we, darling?'

She wasn't so stunned that she couldn't detect the note of warning in his voice. All of a sudden she felt as though she had completely lost the reins on her life. Things were lurching about wildly—a surreal situation that made everything spin around her.

'Well,' her father said, releasing his breath. 'Well, well, well. I don't quite know what to say.' He still looked dazed. 'Of course, I'm stunned; it's all so sudden, isn't it?'

'These things can be unpredictable, can't they, Francesca?' Oliver said lazily, and she threw him her own dazed look.

'Of course,' her father was saying, with some semblance of having re-entered planet Earth, 'your mother and I knew within minutes of meeting that we were meant for one another. I guess it was the same for you.'

'Exactly,' Oliver said smoothly, with a smile in his voice, and Francesca felt faint.

'Well,' her father said again. 'Frankie, darling. Too late, I suppose, to tell you about the birds and the bees? Bit like shutting the door after the proverbial horse has bolted.' She could see that he was coming round to the idea, and she realised with panic that Oliver had been right—the prospect of marriage between them had taken the sting out of the situation. Oliver was a brilliant catch—the biggest fish in the sea—and just the sort of man her father would have wanted for a son-in-law.

He had also put her in an awkward position. How could she tell her father that she didn't want to marry Oliver?

For the next thirty minutes or so she listened with a swirling head while they chatted, but as soon as her father had gone she turned to Oliver and said coldly, 'Thank you very much.'

She stood up and walked across to the huge patio doors and stared, unseeing, out towards the impeccable stretch of manicured lawns. A gardener came twice a week to look after the garden. Her father had once told her that when he'd first been married he had been used to doing a lot of gardening—her mother had loved it—but that when she'd died he'd lost the heart for it.

Francesca had never mowed a lawn in her life.

'I never told you that I wanted to marry you!' she said in a high voice, and the tears were pricking the back of her eyes. 'It's wrong,' she continued, turning around to face him.

He lounged against the mantelpiece, his mouth taut. 'Why? Why is it wrong?'

'You don't love me,' she said bitterly. 'We don't love each other!' Saying that made her wince inside, but she continued to look directly at him. 'People don't get married nowadays for the sake of a baby.'

He walked towards her, taking his time, and there was scathing disgust in his eyes. 'Listen to yourself,' he said tightly. 'Do you really believe that a child should pay for our mistake?'

'No,' Francesca answered, feeling cornered and resenting his implication that she was somehow without morals. 'But you'd end up hating me for having put you in a situation where you felt compelled to marry me,' she said, holding her ground and looking up at him.

'Don't try and analyse me,' he said harshly, and he reached out to hold her shoulders. He looked as though he wanted to shake the living daylights out of her, but she refused to be intimidated.

What would it be like? she thought with despair. Living with him, married to him, bringing up their child, and having to hold her love deep inside her day after day?

'I'm not,' she whispered. 'But it would be a mistake. We have nothing in common.'

'It's too late in the day to start drawing up lists of what we have in common and what we don't,' he said, but the harshness had left his voice and his fingers weren't gripping her quite so fiercely. 'You and that Rupert character had a lot in common. Would you rather the mistake had happened with him?'

'Rupert?' That almost made her laugh. 'I wouldn't have been so stupid.'

Oliver's brows met. 'There's no point debating the issue,' he said shortly. 'Unless, of course, you want to tell your father that you've decided to go it alone.'

'You shouldn't have forced my hand,' Francesca whispered stubbornly.

'Is that what you find most upsetting?' he asked coldly. 'The fact that I forced your hand?'

'No one likes to be pushed into a corner.'

'Life isn't always about doing what you like,' he said in a hard voice, and she felt a rush of tears. She made a helpless, shrugging motion with her shoulders, and he drew her towards the sofa with a sigh.

'Look,' he said, sitting her down and then settling himself next to her and dabbing her streaming eyes with a handkerchief, 'you're going to have to stop finding hidden meanings behind everything I say.'

'I can't,' she said in a trembling voice, taking the handkerchief away from him and doing a better job of wiping her wet face. 'I know how you feel about me. You're critical of me, of everything I represent. I know that life isn't about just picking out the things you like and pretending that unpleasantness doesn't exist, and I know I haven't had much practice at facing lots of things that other people have to face, but I can't bear the thought of being married to you.'

'I see,' he said expressionlessly. 'Why did you make love to me, Francesca?' he asked.

'Because…' she struggled to think of how she could explain it without giving herself and her feelings away in the process. 'Because you're an attractive man.'

'If you really can't face the thought of marrying me, then I won't force you.'

'No.' She tried to feel relieved at that and couldn't.

'But then sit back and try to think clearly of the alternative. Bringing up a baby isn't going to be a piece of cake, however much money your father has.'

'I know that,' she said in a small voice.

'You can look at any marriage we go into as a business arrangement,' he said flatly. 'You may well bitterly regret what's happened, but you should have thought about that before. That fact is that what's happened has happened, and we both have to accept it and do whatever is going to be best for the baby.'

'How can you be so calm about it all?' she demanded in an anguished voice.

'Because I don't see the value in hysterics,' he told her bluntly. 'You're pregnant, I'm the father—and I'm not about to relinquish my responsibilities.'

Francesca listened to him but her thoughts were on herself, on the enormity of raising a baby without help. He'd said that she could consider any marriage they went into as a business arrangement, which said a lot about how he felt about her, but he was right—she wasn't the one at stake here.

'All right,' she said tiredly, defeated. 'I'll marry you.'

'I'll arrange it,' he said, sounding neither relieved nor overjoyed.

'I don't want a big wedding. Dad will try and get us to have a grand affair, but I won't have it. That would be too much of a farce. I just want a register office, and I won't wear white.'

'No one's asking you to,' Oliver murmured, his eyes veiled. 'You can wear screaming scarlet for all I care.'

'Good!' she said, as though she had scored a point.

He stood up and looked down at her. 'Shall I drop you back at your flat?' he asked, and she shook her head slowly.

'I'll stay here for a while,' she said. 'I'll make my own way back.'

He hesitated for a while, but finally he shrugged his shoulders and told her that he'd be in touch on Monday. 'We'll get it all sorted out by the end of next week,' he said, and she gasped and raised her eyes to him. 'Then you'll move in with me. How much notice do you have to give your landlord?'

'Two weeks,' Francesca said, feeling as though she had stepped onto the roller coaster once again. 'But we don't need to move so fast,' she protested faintly.

'Yes, we do. If we don't you'll change your mind every other day and in the long run nothing will be sorted out at all.'

'I wish you wouldn't treat me like an idiot child!' she told him with a burst of energy, and he laughed shortly.

'But that's what you are, isn't it, Francesa? A child who wanted to grow up at the hands of a man she was temporarily attracted to. A child who's finding it difficult to realise that there's such a thing as cause and effect.' He shot her an odd look and then he was gone, and she lay back on the sofa with a sigh of relief.

She wanted to cry again, but what would be the point? So she let her mind go blank and tried to distance herself from the painful thought that Oliver Kemp could give her everything—a ring on her finger, a united family for the baby; he could give her everything but the one thing she wanted. He couldn't give her love.

CHAPTER EIGHT

FRANCESCA hadn't had a great deal of time to think about whether she was doing the right thing or not in getting married. Oliver had come round on Monday evening to her flat and told her that they were going out to dinner.

'What for?' was the first thing she'd asked. He had still been in his business suit—an expensively tailored dark grey double-breasted suit which made him look over-poweringly masculine.

'To have a meal, of course,' he'd said drily. 'Isn't that what most people do when they go out to a restaurant? We need to discuss a few things and we need to eat. It seems a simple enough equation.'

So here they were now, in a cosy French restaurant in Hampstead.

'Have you spoken to your father again about it?' he asked, sipping from a glass of white wine while she toyed with her extremely dull glass of orange juice.

Francesca nodded. 'A lot,' she admitted, contemplating the glass. 'I spent last night there and we talked for hours. I told him that we would be married in a register office, which he wasn't too thrilled about, but he's been fine mostly.'

'He loves you,' Oliver said gently. 'You worked yourself up into a lather wondering what his reaction would be without realising that love can forgive and forget almost anything.'

She didn't want to talk about love. She didn't want to remind herself that that was an emotion which she would have to learn to live without, so she said hurriedly, looking away from those light, penetrating eyes, 'I'm still not sure, though, that we're doing the right thing.'

Their meal came—a fishy affair with lots of creamy sauce—and she fiddled with the attractive array of vegetables, concentrating on her plate rather than on the man sitting opposite her.

'Eat up,' he said, eyeing her lack of enthusiasm for the food, and she glared at him, which made him laugh under his breath.

'I hope you don't intend to order me around when we're married,' she muttered, and he laughed again.

'It would take a brave man to do that, Francesca,' he murmured.

'And what does that mean?'

'It means that you have the sting of a viper.'

'I'm not sure I like that,' she said, frowning, but not feeling as nettled by his remark as she knew she should have—perhaps because there had been a smile in his eyes when he'd said it, and that smile had made her feel warm and foolishly happy.

She began eating, and discovered after a few mouthfuls that she was hungrier than she had thought.

'I've made all the arrangements for the wedding,' he said casually when she had closed her knife and fork on a plate that had been scraped clean. 'Day after tomorrow.'

'Day after tomorrow?' She looked at him, astounded at the speed with which he had moved, and his eyes narrowed.

'No arguments,' he said. 'You can invite a few friends, but the smaller the better, as far as I'm concerned. Then there's the question of our honeymoon.'

'Honeymoon?' Francesca's eyes widened in horror at the thought of that. Honeymoons, she thought, were for lovers, not for two people propelled into marriage by circumstance. 'We don't need a honeymoon,' she said quickly. 'Can't we just get the wedding over and done with and then carry on as normal?'

'You mean as if nothing major had happened?' There was a thread of anger in his voice which puzzled her. 'I realise that you wish you could forget what's happened. It's not a pretty thought to live with, is it—that you jumped into bed with a man purely for physical reasons, and that that one simple, natural action has led to a series of events which you'd like to pretend haven't changed both our lives dramatically?

'But that's what's happened. We're getting married, and we're going to go on a honeymoon. For starters, what do you imagine your father would think if we didn't? He's a conventional man and you've already probably shaken him to his foundations.'

'Oh, so *you've* decided that we need a honeymoon so that we can continue the charade that everything between us is all roses and light.'

'Stop being so damned argumentative,' he rasped. 'You could do with a break abroad somewhere, anyway.'

'I'd prefer—'

'You've already told me what you'd prefer,' he cut in harshly, ignoring the waiter who was hovering at a respectful distance with the dessert menus in his hand. The waiter sidled off and Oliver leaned towards her, his face dark and disturbing.

'We'll spend a week abroad somewhere sunny. The Caribbean, perhaps, or the Far East. Which would you prefer?'

'Oh, the Caribbean, I suppose,' she said with bad grace, and he shot her a dry look.

'Most women would hardly need persuading to take a

holiday in the sun and get away from this filthy British weather that's trying to pass itself off as summer.'

'Well, I'm not most women!'

'No, that you most certainly are not,' he said, looking at her from under his lashes, and she wondered whether this was another little dig, but she decided not to make a point of it. She might as well learn to be civil to him, and to stop cross-examining every little word, every little gesture.

She knew why she did it. She did it because although she didn't regret having given in to that strong, physical impulse to sleep with him, she couldn't forgive herself for her stupidity in having fallen in love with him. For him it was all so much simpler. The woman he was in love with—had been planning to marry—had walked into the sunset with another man, and she, Francesca, had been available—in the right place at the right time.

You could change lots of things in your life, she thought, but the one thing you could never change was your past.

Francesca spent the following day coming to terms with what had happened and what now presented itself on the horizon—a wedding, a honeymoon, a baby in a little over seven months' time. This was reality, and reality had drained her of her youthful optimism and showed her what an utter fool she had been when she had thought that she could hold life in the palm of her hand.

The wedding, in the end, was something of an anticlimax. One minute she was Francesca Wade and the next minute she was Francesca Kemp, and there was ring on her finger, announcing the fact to the world at large.

They had jointly asked a few friends, although her father had made up for the lack by inviting a good few of his own—people who would, he assured her, be devastated if they knew that his only little gem had got married and omitted to include them in the happy event—and after the brief ceremony they went back to her father's house, where, frustrated by the lack of a grand affair, he had laid on an elaborate buffet.

Amongst the guests were Imogen and Rupert, and Francesca did her best to avoid looking at Imogen, because every time she did she wondered what was going on in Oliver's head when he looked at the woman he had lost to someone else.

She didn't want to surprise any unguarded looks of longing for what might have been if things had turned out differently. But the effort of averting her eyes and pretending that she was happy made her feel stiff and miserable.

'Cheer up,' Oliver ordered *sotto voce*, with his arm around her, and she replied without looking at him.

'I'm smiling as hard as I can.'

'I know. I can tell.'

'No one else has noticed anything,' she pointed out. There was a lot of laughing going on, and easy conversation, and her father was having a great time strutting around proudly.

'No,' he said under his breath, 'but I'm learning to pick up signals from you.' He kept his arm around her, and it was only when the party was beginning to disperse that she found herself face to face with Imogen.

'I've hardly had a chance to talk to you,' the other woman said, drawing her to one side and sitting her down. There was a warm smile on her lips and Francesca tried to respond in kind. She felt tired and sleepy. Pregnancy seemed to have made her feel permanently tired. What she would really have liked was to be able to sleep for the next few months and awaken only when the baby was due to be born, conveniently skipping the intervening period which threatened to be to a slow version of the Chinese water torture.

'I've been rushed off my feet,' Francesca said vaguely. Apart from her father no one as yet knew that she was pregnant. She still had her slim, coltish figure, and maternity dresses seemed a long way away as yet.

'It all happened so quickly, didn't it?' Imogen agreed, smiling. 'Bit like Rupert and myself. We're planning on getting married later on this year, and I shall be giving up my job to start a family and to help Rupert run the estate.

'I've already warned him that he's got to get used to staying in, because when a screaming baby comes along yours truly isn't going to be cooped up in his rambling manor looking after it all by herself!' She laughed and Francesca joined in, feeling a pang of envy at the thought of the blissful family life that awaited the other girl.

'I'm happy for Oliver as well,' Imogen said confidentially, her face sobering. 'We were so close, and I hated to think that what happened between us might have jaded his faith in the opposite sex.'

'Don't you feel a little bit...?' Francesca sought around for the right words to convey her curiosity.

Imogen helpfully said, 'Aggrieved? Not desperately. For a while I had felt that it would be something of a mistake to marry Oliver, but I couldn't put my finger on it so I drifted along with the idea. I only realised what was missing when I fell in love with Rupert.

'It's a bit like my career, I suppose. I always did very well academically, and I had a great deal of luck along the way. I got a good job from the start and found myself being promoted until I'd reached the pinnacle of success.' She shrugged. 'I shan't be too sorry to give it all up.'

Francesca looked at her thoughtfully, and then said, 'Would you and Oliver have had children, do you think, if you had married?'

'Oh, yes.' Rupert was beckoning to her from across the room, holding up his wrist and pointing to his watch theatrically.

She stood up and then said casually, laughing, 'Oliver's always wanted a family. I think he would have done anything to have had a child straight away. He didn't want to wait until he was too old. I think it affected him more than he liked to admit—the fact that both his parents died when he was relatively young. He wanted to make sure that he was around to see his children into middle age.' She laughed again. 'Not that there's ever any certainty about that!'

The guests were beginning to depart, and Francesca did her duty and waved them off with a smile on her face, but she understood better now why Oliver had propelled her into marriage. He moved across to her and put his arm around her. The happy couple, she thought; at least to the outside world. No one would ever guess in a million years that all of this was an elaborate charade, performed because of what lay inside her.

They left soon after for the airport, and in the car Francesca lay back with her eyes closed, not saying anything, thinking.

When Oliver had made love to her that night it had been because he had wanted her. And he had needed the warmth of another body next to his. Whatever he said, the more she heard, the more she realised that if Rupert had never come along Imogen would still have been the woman with his ring on her finger.

Doubtless, for all her silly hopes at the time, his desire

would have waned rapidly, because essentially what he had wanted had not been *her* but simply an attractive woman to tide him through a difficult period. They weren't on the same wavelength. That had always been what he'd thought, and he still thought that.

But the pregnancy had changed everything. It had transformed an ill-fated night of passion into a lifelong obligation.

She glanced across at his profile and knew that she would never have guessed how strong his desire for a child was if his ex-girlfriend hadn't obligingly provided the information. Everyone, she supposed, had their own peculiar vulnerability.

She closed her eyes, and the next time she opened them they were at the airport and he was shaking her gently by the shoulder to make her wake up, which she did, with a wide yawn and as effective a stretch as she could manage within the confines of a car.

'Ready?' he asked, with a grin in his voice. 'Or shall I carry the suitcases and put you on the trolley so that you can continue your nap?'

'It's not my fault,' she answered irritably, yawning again. 'It's the hormones.' At which he laughed outright and raised his eyebrows in a dry question.

'And how long will these hormones be responsible for whatever you do?' he asked, and she stole a sideways look at him. He looked relaxed and sexy. Very sexy. He had changed out of his charcoal suit into a pair of dark green trousers and an oatmeal-coloured shirt which made him look alarmingly handsome.

'Months,' she said, clicking open the door and throwing over her shoulder, 'Maybe years.'

He was still grinning when he emerged from the driver's seat.

The airport was crowded but not unduly so. They were travelling out of the peak period.

Oliver handled everything with the self-assurance of someone who was accustomed to going abroad, and he was treated with the exaggerated respect paid to first-class travellers.

Francesca simply skulked in the background, watching the toing and froing of everyone else, and wondering whether she was the only one in the airport who wasn't overjoyed at the thought of leaving the country.

It was an eight-hour flight and she was dreading it, but in the end she slept through most of it, and when she was awake she found herself reluctantly beginning to enjoy the prospect of a week in the sun.

They stepped off the plane into blazing sunshine. It was some time since Francesca had been to the Caribbean. She had forgotten how vivid the colours were. Everything had an unreal brightness about it. The greens of the trees were somehow greener, the flowers brighter, the sky flawlessly blue. And the heat was of a kind rarely experienced in England. It made you feel lazy and peaceful.

She had worn light clothes, but by the time they made it to the hotel she was perspiring and dying for a shower.

It was only when they were shown to their room that she remembered, with a jolt of alarm, that this was a honeymoon and that they would be sharing a bed. She had half forgotten that she was married, just as she had half forgotten what marriage from now on would entail.

She eyed the double bed warily from the door and Oliver said drily, stripping off his shirt, 'Stop hovering. You look as though you're about to be eaten.' He disappeared into the bathroom without bothering to shut the door, and she hurriedly began unpacking her stuff and ignoring the bed.

When he emerged he was naked except for a towel loosely draped over his waist, and she snapped awkwardly, 'Couldn't you have dressed?'

He stopped where he was and gave her a long look, then he moved very slowly towards her.

'Has it slipped your mind that we're married now, Francesca?' he asked with icy politeness. The relaxed charm that had been on his face less than an hour ago had vanished.

'In name only,' she retorted, and his dark eyebrows met in an angry frown.

'Is that what you think?'

'What else should I think? We both know that the only reason we're here is because of the baby, and now that there's no one else around I don't see why we have to continue pretending.'

The colour had risen to her cheeks, partly because she was as heated as he was, but mostly because he was standing so close to her. If she stretched her hand out only a little she would touch that hard, powerful torso. Not knowing what stupid impulse she might give in to, she stuck her hands behind her back and looked up at him.

'What do you suggest we do?' he asked softly, but there was a dangerous silkiness in his voice that made her shiver.

'We could go our separate ways,' she suggested nervously, looking away.

'And occasionally meet in passing in the restaurant?'

She didn't answer, and he reached out and caught her arm in his fingers.

'Now you listen to me,' he said in a very controlled voice. 'We're married. You can analyse the reasons behind it until you go blue in the face but that doesn't change a thing, and, believe me, I have no intention of not coming near you whenever there's no one around looking.'

'Wh-what do you mean?' she stammered.

'I mean, this is going to be a marriage in every sense of the word.' He paused, giving her time for that to sink in, and she looked at him with dismay.

'You can't mean that,' she said.

'Every word. If you think marriage between us is going to mean sharing the same roof while I go my own way with other women, then you're wrong.'

'So you're going to be faithful, are you, Oliver?' she asked tightly. 'To a woman whom you don't love? You expect me to believe that?'

'I have no doubt that you'll believe exactly what you want to believe.'

'And you don't care! And what about when temptation positions itself in front of you?'

He looked at her with a perplexed frown. 'What on earth are you rambling on about now?'

'Helen?' She felt quite wretched but took great pains not to show it. 'Helen Scott? You gave her my job without even telling me! What else did you give her?'

His lips thinned. 'You little fool! Is that what that troublemaker told you? She isn't working for me! Why do you blindly believe whatever you're told? Sometimes I feel I could wring your neck, woman! Now, shut up and look at me.'

She raised her eyes to his face and her pulses gave a leap.

'Go ahead,' he said in a rough voice. 'Touch me.'

'No. I can't.'

'Yes, you can.' His mouth twisted into a dry smile. 'You think that if you disassociate yourself from me you can pretend that nothing's happened, but you're still attracted to me, Francesca, aren't you?' His voice had sunk to a mocking drawl that brought a flush of colour to her cheeks.

'No, I'm not,' she lied, staring into his wintry eyes with an odd sense of animal panic. 'I hate myself for what's happened. I gave in to one crazy impulse and it wrecked my life. I know that we're married now, but I don't want anything to do with you.'

'What do you think is going to happen if you give in to me again?' he asked softly, tilting her chin up with his fingers so that she was forced to look at him. 'Do you think that the heavens are going to fall down on you?'

'I don't want to talk about this,' she whispered. 'It's pointless, all this talk.'

'Like it or not, we're going to have to talk about it,' Oliver said in a hard voice. 'You've never had to face anything unpleasant in your whole life, have you, Francesca? That's why you're finding it so difficult to face this.'

'Would Imogen handle the situation any better?' she asked bitterly. 'You're so eager to point out what a hopeless failure I am. Is that because you're measuring me against impossible standards? I'll never be like your ex-girlfriend.'

'Have I ever told you that you're a hopeless failure?' he asked with curiosity. His senses had sharpened, and she knew that she would have to tread carefully, or else she could very easily end up revealing much more than she wanted to.

'You implied it,' she muttered. 'I know I've had a privileged background. I can't help that.'

'Are you jealous of Imogen?' he asked. 'Just like you were jealous of Helen Scott? What do you think that means?'

She pulled away from him and walked across to the bedroom window.

She had known that he was going to ask her that. She should never have brought Imogen into the conversation at all, just as she shouldn't have mentioned Helen. But she hadn't been able to prevent herself. She was blindly jealous. Helen, she realised now, was no more than a mischief-maker, but Imogen would always be a lurking threat.

'Well?' he asked, coming up behind her. 'Answer me.'

'Are you jealous of Rupert?' she asked him back, avoiding the question.

'You weren't engaged to Rupert,' he reminded her smoothly. 'Nor had you ever slept with him.'

She was glad that she wasn't looking at him, glad that she was staring in an unfocused manner at the stretch of lawns outside, because that meant that he couldn't see the play of strong emotion on her face.

'And if I had?' she asked quietly.

'That's a hypothetical question.'

'Pretend that it isn't.'

'All right.' He paused, and she wondered what was going through his mind. 'I can't be jealous of a man so obviously unsuited to you. If you had been engaged to him, it would only have been a matter of time before you came to your senses.' She felt rather than heard him turn away. 'Go and have your shower, Francesca, and then get some sleep.'

'Yes, I think I will.' She walked across to the bed, collected some clothes and headed for the bathroom, making sure that she didn't look at him *en route*. She felt drained—utterly drained.

She took a long shower, and when she emerged half an hour later Oliver was no longer in the room. He had cleared the clothes from the bed, and she opened one of the drawers to find them neatly stacked away in separate little disordered bundles, which brought a reluctant smile to her lips. She cleared the lot out, folded them all, put them away again, then thought that she'd never get to sleep, but did as soon as her head hit the pillow.

Francesca opened her eyes to see Oliver standing over her in a pair of tan shorts and a T-shirt, and there was a wry smile on his mouth.

'How long have you been there?' she asked, sitting up and rubbing her eyes. 'Hovering. It's bad manners to hover.'

She felt better for the sleep. With a shock she realised that she had more than slept the clock round. She hadn't thought that she was particularly tired, but she must have been because she had been dead to the world for such a long time.

'You redid all my unpacking,' he said, lightly teasing, sitting on the bed next to her and depressing it with his weight. 'What was wrong with my efforts?'

'You're supposed to fold things neatly before you put them away,' she said, still feeling drowsy, and rather liking the way he was sitting there on the bed next to her when she didn't stop to think about it.

'Ah.' He nodded. 'Thank you for sharing that with me. I can honestly say that that will change the course of my life.'

She laughed, and then asked suspiciously, 'Why are you being so nice?'

'Isn't it easier than being nasty?' he quipped, which made her grin again, though warily. 'Now, come along,' he said, in the voice of someone hustling along a young child. 'The world is waiting outside for you—swimming pools, strange-looking plants, warm blue sea, white sand, lunch.'

'Lunch,' she said, slipping past him off the bed and heading towards the bathroom to change. 'I'm starved.'

She slammed the bathroom door behind her and had a bit of a do trying to get into her shorts, which were already too tight for her. She managed to zip them up, but only just, and she realised ruefully that tight waistbands were now more or less out of the question.

'Lunch on the beach, I thought,' he said as they left the room and headed outside, which seemed a wonderful idea to her. She stole a sideways glance at him from under her lashes and felt that familiar quickening of her senses.

He was right. There was no sense in being antagonistic towards one another, circling each other like adversaries. It was a great deal less effort and a great deal less wearing on the nerves to be pleasant.

'Sounds marvellous,' she said politely.

They walked through the gardens, past the turquoise swimming pool with its faithful cluster of semi-clad bodies stretched out on sun-loungers, past bright green hedges interspersed with brilliant red flowers, then down a few steps towards the beach—eight uneven, steep stone steps, and he turned around and held her hand, the gesture without any sexual undertones.

'There,' he said, turning to face her. 'What do you think?'

'Gorgeous, isn't it,' she said, looking from one end of the long beach to the other. The water was calm, almost without ripple, and blue—the sort of perfect aquamarine blue that you saw in photographs and suspected of being touched up here and there. There were a few sun-loungers with people lazily dozing on them, a few towels laid out on the white sand, but really it was virtually empty.

They walked towards a small round table, shaded underneath an umbrella which seemed to grow out of its centre like one of the bright flowers they had passed along the way. Behind them and a little to the right was a bar, with a barman incongruously kitted out in a red and black outfit, and a chef, also incongruously kitted out in a white chef's uniform and a chef's hat.

Francesca pulled one of the sun-loungers towards her, stretched out on it with a towel behind her head, closed her eyes and told Oliver that he could order her whatever he wanted to for lunch.

'I could eat a horse,' she said, wishing that she had brought a straw hat with her.

'I'll find out what kind they do,' he said seriously from above her, and she smiled. 'And cover your face with something,' he continued. 'You'll end up the colour of a lobster otherwise.' He tossed a newspaper over her, which made her yelp in surprise, but she took his advice and put it over her face so that it blocked out the sun.

She felt lazy and relaxed. It was the sun, of course. The warmth had the same effect as a glass of good wine. It made you feel mellow and easygoing. She lay perfectly still in her bikini, wondering if this was what a piece of bread felt like when it went into a toaster.

'Don't tell me the hormones are sending you to sleep again,' she heard him say in a lazy drawl.

'Sun and hormones are a bad combination,' she informed him, not bothering to take the newspaper off her face.

'Come on,' he said.

'Come on where?' She lifted the newspaper and peered at him. He was pulling a lounger towards a clump of coconut trees.

'Somewhere a bit quieter,' he said, returning and waving

her off the chair so that he could do the same with hers. She followed him, clutching her bag with her suntan cream and dark glasses.

'Food will be ready in about fifteen minutes,' he said, pulling his T-shirt over his head. 'Two horse burgers and chips.'

'Very healthy,' Francesca said, laughing. For some peculiar reason she felt suddenly very shy with him. 'We don't want to start getting the baby into bad eating habits, do we?'

Their eyes met and there was the briefest of silences—a silence charged with all sorts of meanings, but mostly with that bond between them that lay there inside her—then he said in an oddly rough voice, 'We most certainly don't. We can't have a baby screaming for a plate of cholesterol the minute she comes out of the womb.'

Francesca smiled again, but she felt slightly unsteady. For perhaps the first time she had thought of the baby not as the catalyst to a host of problems but as a miracle growing inside her.

'Now lie down,' he ordered. 'On your stomach. While you still can.'

'What are you going to do?'

He didn't answer. He squeezed some lotion out of one of the tubes and she lay down, half closing her eyes as he began to spread the suntan cream over her, his hands moving slowly and rhythmically—first her shoulders, then along her back, along her waist, then down to her thighs and legs. There was nothing sensual in what he was doing, but a delicious sensation of contentment began spreading through her.

The sun was making her fuzzy-headed, she thought languorously. It was so hot that even thinking of bristling at him for what he was doing made her feel tired.

'Right,' he said. 'Turn over.'

She wriggled onto her back and lay with her arms hanging down on either side. When she opened her eyes she could see the slight swell of her stomach—noticeable, she knew, only to her because she was looking for it—and his dark head, as he began spreading the lotion along her feet.

When his hands began their rhythmic movements along her thighs she knew that her breathing had quickened and that a moist awareness of him was spreading through her. She shifted so that her legs were closer together, but his hands were already working their way upwards over her stomach.

'You're beginning to put on some weight,' he said in a surprised voice. 'I hadn't noticed before.'

'It only shows because I'm wearing this,' Francesca answered self-consciously.

There was an intimacy now in what he was doing which she hadn't noticed there before. Or perhaps, she thought, she was imagining it. She looked towards the snack bar to see whether the chef was bustling his way across to them, but no one was coming, and in this secluded little area they were virtually unnoticed. Lower down, towards the sea, odd couples occasionally strolled by, but they hardly glanced in their direction.

'It suits you,' he said, circling her stomach with his hands, not looking at her face. 'Makes you look more rounded.'

The sun, pouring through the fronds of the palm trees above them, threw a dappled pattern over him which moved every time he did. Francesca could not tear her eyes away from the dance of sun and shade on his body. She felt spellbound.

He squirted some more cream onto the palm of his hand and worked his way over her ribcage.

'Your breasts are fuller too,' he remarked in the same slightly surprised voice.

Their eyes met, and in the peaceful rustle of the breeze she could hear her own breathing—soft and quick, like a gentle panting.

'Where on earth has our lunch gone?' she asked, in a desperate attempt to break the fascination he held her in, but she couldn't tear her eyes away from his, and it was no surprise when his hands moved to massage the roundness of her breasts, which were pushing against the flimsy material of the bikini top. She could feel her nipples harden and swell under his manipulation, aching for the rub of his fingers over them.

'Oliver…' she said, on a small, protesting sigh.

'Oliver, what?' he asked, smiling crookedly at her. 'Oliver, keep doing what you're doing? Oliver, I want you to make love to me?'

He trailed his finger along her cleavage and then outlined the throbbing contours of her nipples, taking his time.

'Oliver, stop,' she said weakly. She glanced across and sat up. 'Here comes our food.'

He laughed and followed the direction of her eyes. 'Saved by the bell,' he said lightly, mockingly, and she ignored him, waiting until their food had been deposited in front of them—two oversized beefburgers which smelt wonderful, enough chips to keep several people happy, and two tall, very cold, very colourful drinks, with a piece of pineapple wedged over the rim of each glass.

Her body still felt as though it was on fire, as though it had been denied something which it had desperately craved.

She looked at him—a quick, veiled look—and wondered how she was ever going to fight this man who had been her lover, and was now her husband.

CHAPTER NINE

FRANCESCA knew precisely what was going on in Oliver's head. Or at least she felt that she could make a pretty accurate stab at it.

They were now husband and wife, and even though he wasn't in love with her he saw no reason why he shouldn't sleep with her. He had been at his most charming during the day—so charming, in fact, that it was difficult to believe that there was so much going on underneath that veneer of civilised pretence.

Because that, she felt, was what it was. This, she thought, was all very well for him, but what about her? She could see herself sinking ever deeper into the quagmire of her emotions if she let him make love to her, and then one day, probably in the not too distant future, when he had tired of making love to her, he would look at her and realise that, baby or no baby, he could never love her, and where would she be then?

He had told her that as far as he was concerned he intended their marriage to be much more than just a marriage on paper, but she knew with a sense of foreboding that no marriage could survive without the bond of love. It was a realisation that would come to him over time.

Being married to him would legitimise their baby, but it left her floundering in a frightening sort of limbo, too scared to commit even more than she already had, but equally scared that her feelings for him ran too deep for her to resist the pull of his attraction.

She felt torn between the devil and the deep blue sea,

not knowing what stand she could take, and too inexperienced even to begin to know how to tackle the problem.

If she were ten years older, she might have accumulated enough knowledge of the opposite sex along the way to enable her to treat their relationship with the same adult cynicism as he obviously treated it. But she wasn't. She could look back now and see how hopelessly naïve she had been to make her attraction to him so patently clear.

She had never slept with a man before, and her boy-friends had been playmates rather than anything serious. Temptation had been something she had never had to tackle, so when it had presented itself to her she had reacted in what she realised now to have been the worst possible way—she'd yielded.

Was it any wonder that Oliver couldn't see why there should be any physical barriers between them now? How was he to know that the reason she had made love to him in the first place had been because he meant so much to her—so much more than a transient, pleasurable flirtation?

She stood in the middle of the room, with the balmy ink-black night pressing against the windows, lost in thought, frowning, and she jumped when he said in a rough, mildly impatient voice, 'What's the matter with you now?'

She looked up to find him staring at her, and there was amused irritation on his face.

'Nothing's the matter,' she said hastily, which she feebly hoped might put an end to the conversation. 'I was just thinking,' she continued nervously.

He sighed and walked towards her, and she had to steel herself not to start backing away, or, worse, to rush towards him and bury herself in his arms.

'You,' he said, 'are the most moody, most bloody illogical person I have ever met in my entire life. Ten minutes ago you were laughing downstairs with me and now you're acting as though Judgement Day is just around the corner.' He put his hands on her shoulders and she froze.

There wasn't a bed downstairs, she wanted to inform him.

'Am I?' She tried a laugh. 'It's just that I seem to have developed a headache.'

'Oh, really?' he said drily. 'Surely you can do better than that, Francesca?'

'I have got a headache,' she insisted irritably. 'You talk about me reading hidden meanings behind everything you say. Well, why can't you take what I tell you at face value?'

'Because nothing you say is meant at face value,' he told her, idly massaging her shoulders with his hands. 'Nothing on a personal level at any rate. You can chat happily enough about books and music and the scenery, but the minute we get onto anything remotely personal your thought processes seem to take a nosedive.'

'I am not an irrational child, Oliver. I'm a woman carrying a baby!'

'Only here.' He touched her stomach with the flat palm of his hand and she felt herself shudder convulsively. He felt the quiver of her body and laughed under his breath. 'And here,' he murmured, dropping his hand further to feel the outline of her womanhood through her thin, floaty skirt.

She pulled away from him and snapped, 'This isn't a game, you know.'

'I know that.' His mouth tightened and he watched as she walked towards the window and began drawing the curtains together. She felt as though she had to do something—anything—to break the crackle of electricity that had sprung up between them. She wrapped her arms around herself and turned to face him, with her back pressed against the window-ledge.

'I can't sleep with you. I just can't,' she said, in a voice that wanted to be strong and firm, but had enough of a plea in it to make his brows snap together in a frown.

'Why not?' he asked bluntly.

'I wouldn't be able to face myself if I did; I'd hate myself,' Francesca answered quietly. 'I know you probably can't understand this. I know what I'm saying doesn't make a scrap of sense to you because we've already slept together, and it's a bit late in the day to start having scruples, especially since I'm carrying your baby, but—'

'But you slept with me once,' he grated harshly, 'and thought that everything would be wonderful afterwards and it wasn't. Is that it?'

'Something like that,' she admitted nervously. 'We both did things for the wrong reasons, maybe,' she floundered on, 'but that doesn't mean that we have to keep on committing the same mistake.'

'So, in other words, I'm to expect that our marriage won't be consummated?'

Put like that, she could see why he was beginning to show the stirrings of anger, but she maintained a long silence and refused to be browbeaten by that sharp mind of his, which could outmatch anything she could hope to come up with.

'You don't want me anyway, Oliver, not really. The woman you want is Imogen. You just happen to have landed yourself with me.'

'Leave Imogen out of this!' he roared, and she glanced quickly and apprehensively towards the door.

'Look at me,' he commanded, walking towards her, his body swift and graceful. 'Look at me, in the face, and tell me that you're not attracted to me.'

He touched her face, and although there was anger in his voice his fingers were strangely tender, caressing. Her breathing quickened, and she looked down, concentrating her attention on the gleaming floorboards.

'That's hardly the point,' she muttered under her breath. 'Sleeping with someone just because you happen to be attracted to them is an animal instinct.'

'You make desire sound like a sin, Francesca. And we're not talking about sleeping with just anyone, are we? We're married now.'

'Unfortunately.'

He swore under his breath and said evenly, keeping his temper in check, 'I'm going to have a shower. I won't force you into anything, rest assured. You may be a desirable woman, Francesca, but your desirability has its limits.'

'Yes, I know that.' She could have told him that desire always had its limits. It burnt like a fire and then died out, because without love there was never enough to sustain it indefinitely.

She didn't look at him as he walked away towards the bathroom and shut the door quietly between them.

But as soon as the room was empty she quickly undressed and slipped on her nightgown—a Victorian affair of white lace which made her feel like a prim little virgin, but which she had had for years and was comfortable.

She was half-asleep when she felt him slip into the bed next to her, and she tensed immediately, wide awake now, wondering whether he would try and force his point home, try and make her admit to him just how much she wanted him, but he didn't. He turned away from her, and she waited for what seemed like ages, her eyes getting heavier and heavier until she was too tired to be tense, too tired to care whether his even breathing meant that he was asleep...

It was a little after three in the morning when she woke up. She knew that because the first thing she saw was the illuminated digital face of the travel clock on the little cabinet next to her bed.

Then she realised drowsily that the reason she had awakened was because Oliver's arm was slung over her body—a warm weight which she tried to wriggle free of. But wriggling only brought her closer to him. He was pressed against her with her back curved against his chest. She moved again and his arm tightened around her, but it was a reflex reaction, she knew, because his breathing was still deep and regular, and very gradually she turned around to face him so that she could free herself of the inviting pressure of his body.

It was only when she looked up that she saw that his eyes were open and he was looking at her, his face almost invisible in the darkness in the bedroom.

She gasped in shock and said unsteadily, 'You're awake.' Brilliant observation, she thought crossly to herself.

'So I am,' he said, moving his arm and preparing to turn away from her.

'It's cold in here,' she said, and immediately wondered why she was prolonging a conversation at three in the morning.

'Would you like me to switch the air-conditioning off?' Oliver asked, inclining his body slightly so that he was facing her once again, his voice polite.

'No. It'll get too hot, and I don't want to have the windows open. The mosquitoes can be vicious over here.'

'OK.'

'Did you bring any insect repellent?'

'No. Why are we having this conversation at this ridiculous hour of the morning?'

She didn't know. She just knew that she had liked the feel of his body next to hers and that she wanted to have the weight of it against her again. It was comforting.

'It wasn't a conversation, it was a simple question.'

'Well, this is an extremely odd time to start a question-and-answer game,' he replied. 'So goodnight. If I get too close to you again just shove me off.' His voice was cool but held no anger.

'Oliver...'

'What is it now?'

I wish I knew, she thought. I want you, she thought. I don't care about tomorrow, she thought; I just know that I can't spend my nights with you without touching that magnificent body of yours, without feeding my addiction.

She reached out and ran her hand along his side, realising with heightened excitement that he wasn't wearing anything, and she felt him stiffen under the slight caress.

He caught her hand in his and said coldly, 'Now is not the time for games like this.'

'I'm not playing a game,' she said huskily.

'You don't know what you're doing. One minute you're fighting me tooth and nail, and the next minute you want me to make love to you. It won't do, Francesca. I'm not some damned boy who's going to patiently indulge your whims.'

'No, you're not a boy,' she whispered unsteadily. She wriggled a bit closer and placed her mouth over his, running her tongue along his lips, darting it inside his mouth, but he didn't respond. He tightened his grip on her and she drew back.

'What's happened to all this self-hatred you claimed you would feel if you laid a hand on me?' he asked icily, and she didn't answer. He let her go. 'Have you decided in the warmth of a bed, with darkness all around, that you can live with yourself after all?' There was enough of a sneer in his voice to bring the tears glistening to her eyes.

'I didn't think about it at all,' she said.

'That's your problem, though, isn't it?'

She turned away from him in blind anger and slipped off the bed.

She really hadn't thought anything except that she wanted him quite desperately, that she needed to reach out and touch him, and his rejection was like a slap in the face. It hurt.

'Where are you going, dammit?' He sat up, expecting her to vanish into the bathroom, no doubt, she thought, but she suddenly needed time to get her thoughts in order.

She felt utterly confused, like someone who had been whirling around on a roller coaster and now felt the need to step off so that her mind could catch up with her body.

She knew what she had told him, but logic and reason had played no part in the shared intimacy of a darkened bedroom. She wanted to protect herself, but was there any point in the end? Was there any point in playing the martyr, in waiting for the inevitable axe to fall on their relationship? Was the dubious benefit of knowing that he had no idea of how she really felt really worth the misery of denying herself the one thing that could bring her happiness, even if it was only temporary happiness?

The questions soared through her mind, like a jigsaw puzzle that had been splintered into a thousand pieces. She felt that if only she could put the pieces together she could arrive at a solution.

'I need to think,' she said in a high voice, and he only began to get out of bed when he realised that she was leaving the room.

She ran, imagining him as he sprinted towards the light switch and began chaotically throwing on some clothes, and her imagination made her run faster, through the reception area, which was quiet and empty, out into the gardens and down towards the beach.

Outside it was warm, the air heavy, and around her she picked up all the small sounds of the night life—crickets, frogs, insects which she could not put a name to but which called to each other in the night from bush to bush.

She looked around and saw nothing, and ran faster, her legs flying over the grass and her white nightgown billowing around her. The long nightdress which had seemed protective in the dangerous confines of the bedroom now seemed positively useless, and she gathered up the bottom, bunching the cloth in her fist.

In the pitch-blackness of the night she saw the strip of sea and headed towards it, knowing that the beach would give her the silence she needed to think things through.

She took one last look behind her, and saw Oliver racing towards her—a silent, swift-moving figure, covering the distance between them like an arrow. She knew that he would have seen her as well, but he didn't call out. It seemed somehow inappropriate to shout into the stillness of the night.

Francesca turned round, stepped forward, and felt herself falling down the stone steps in what appeared to be an agony of slow motion.

In daylight the steps had been uneven and steep. At night they were treacherous.

She lay at the bottom in a heap, unable to move, and closed her eyes, waiting for Oliver to arrive. It didn't take him long. When she opened her eyes she looked up to see him towering at the top of the steps, then he sprinted down to her.

'Are you all right?' he asked, his voice urgent. He tried to help her up and she gave a little moan of pain.

'I can't move,' she whispered.

'You little fool. What did you think you were doing, running off like that? Where do you hurt? Is it your leg? Have you twisted your ankle?' He didn't wait for her to answer. He scooped her up very gently, like a child, and slowly carried her up the steps back towards the hotel.

She closed her eyes and clung to him, hearing voices in a blur. He was talking to someone, his voice quick and commanding.

'We're going to get you to a doctor,' he said to her. 'Don't worry, you're going to be all right.'

'I didn't see the steps,' Francesca whimpered. 'I knew they were there, but I lost my footing on the top one and there was nothing to hold onto.'

He carried her across to a sofa in the reception area and sat down, still cradling her.

'I'll be all right,' she told him in a weak voice. 'There's no need to get a doctor out. It can wait until the morning.' She felt dreadful, bruised all over, but, more than that, there was a wrenching ache in her stomach, and her mind veered away from what that might mean.

'Listen to me, Francesca,' he said, gently and firmly. 'You're bleeding very slightly, and it won't wait until the morning. I've sent the receptionist off to get the hotel doctor. He only lives about fifteen minutes away from here. He'll be here shortly.'

'What do you mean, I'm bleeding?' She felt tears welling up into her eyes and she tried to sit up, but he held her against him.

'Francesca,' he said after a while, with a rough edge to his voice, 'I...I'm sorry. Dammit, this is all my fault.'

She opened her eyes to look at him. 'I shouldn't have

run off like that,' she mumbled, and he put his finger over her lips, but although his face was as controlled as ever his finger trembled slightly.

The doctor arrived, took one look at her and told Oliver to follow him. He had a small but comprehensive office on the ground floor and they walked there in silence.

Through Oliver's shirt she could hear the beating of his heart—a rapid thud against her ears—and she had an over-powering desire to stay where she was, held close against him, because there was something so strong and reassuring about him. She felt safe. Ironic, she thought. It was thanks to him that her life was in the mess that it was, but right now she knew that no one could give her the comfort that he did.

'So what happened here, young lady?' the doctor asked, indicating to Oliver where to put her down.

Francesca looked at the small, wiry man, with his dark, intelligent face and said, 'I'm very sorry to have got you out of bed at this hour in the morning.'

'I wouldn't have become a doctor if I wasn't prepared for these sorts of things,' he said, his eyes busily register-ing her bruises while his fingers gently pressed her body.

'I understand you're pregnant,' he said, and she nodded. 'I'll want to examine you to make sure that everything is OK.' He looked at Oliver. 'You'll stay?' he asked, in a voice that implied that his presence in the room was taken for granted, and Oliver nodded quietly, holding her hand, brushing her hair away from her face.

She clung to his hand. Things seemed to have happened so quickly. One minute they were in the bedroom, and she was feeling that urgent, restless need to silence the thoughts in her head which were clamouring and driving her mad, and the next minute she was falling down those steps, feeling every little bump along the way, powerless to do anything to protect herself.

It hadn't been at all like tripping down a staircase. She had fallen down stairs once before, when she was fifteen. She had been at school, looking back over her shoulder, laughing, saying something to the girl behind her, and she had missed her footing and fallen, but it hadn't been serious because she had been able to hang onto the banister as soon as her legs gave way.

As soon as she had felt herself falling down the steps to the beach she had known that she had no option but to continue falling until she reached the bottom.

The doctor was asking her questions and she answered them, but listlessly. She felt as though she had exhausted her reserves of energy. Eventually, he straightened up and his face was serious.

'You've had an awkward fall, young lady. No broken bones, which is good, but you're bleeding and there's some possibility that you might miscarry this baby.'

It was what she had been dreading. Hearing your suspicions put into words was always awful because it made them real—it took away the little seed of hope that perhaps you were wrong, that perhaps you were imagining it all. She groaned and squeezed her eyes tightly shut.

She heard Oliver ask sharply, 'What do you mean a *possibility*? Can't you be more certain than that?'

Francesca wished that she could close her ears to what they were saying. She didn't want to hear. She wanted to be an ostrich and stick her head in the sand, but she couldn't. All she could hear was their voices, obliterating everything else.

'Normally a fall in pregnancy is nothing to worry about,' the doctor was saying in a detached but sympathetic voice. 'The baby is well cushioned inside the amniotic sac, but sometimes, if the fall is awkward, it can precipitate a miscarriage. Your wife is bleeding, but we won't know anything for sure until she's had a scan.'

'Now,' Oliver said harshly. 'We want a scan now, this instant.'

The doctor said gently, 'It's impossible. I will arrange for you to take her to the hospital first thing in the morning.' He began packing his little black bag. Doctors always carried little black bags, she thought inconsequentially. Why not red, or green? Or purple?

He wrote on a piece of paper and handed it to Oliver.

'You'll see a Dr Girot,' he said. 'I'll call him so that he knows to expect you. In the meantime—' he looked at Francesca and gave her arm a small, reassuring squeeze '—no more night-time saunters to the beach, young lady. You go up to your bedroom and stay put. I've left my number with your good husband here; he can call me any time if you're worried, it's in the good Lord's hands now.'

It was nearly five by the time they got back up to the bedroom. Dawn was beginning to glimmer over the horizon. In three hours' time the hotel would be bustling once again with tourists going in and out, preparing themselves for another hard day of doing absolutely nothing under the baking hot sun.

Oliver placed her on the bed and she watched him, not quite knowing what to say. He stripped off his shirt, which had been haphazardly buttoned, and tossed it onto the chair by the dressing-table, then he sat on the bed next to her with an unreadable expression on his face.

'You've got to try and get some sleep, Francesca,' he said.

'I can't. How can I sleep?'

The doctor had given her two mild painkillers for her bruises, which felt sore and throbbing.

'I was a fool,' she said dully. 'You're right. I don't think before I act. Nobody else—' Imogen, for instance, she thought, with a twinge of pain '—would have rushed out of the room and ended up tripping down eight steps to the beach.'

'Stop whipping yourself. It's done. We just have to wait and see what happens in the morning.'

'If I lose this baby, it'll never be done for me.' She fiddled with her fingers, anxiously clasping and unclasping them, and he reached out and placed his hand over hers, stilling the worried little movements.

'Don't think the worst,' he said gruffly, but she could tell from the tone of his voice that he had already thought of that outcome himself.

'I have to. We both do.' She raised her eyes and looked at him evenly. 'We got married for the sake of the baby, and if there's no baby...' She paused because she knew that if she carried on her voice would break. 'If there's no baby,' she continued, taking a deep breath, 'then what's the point of the marriage?'

He didn't say a word. He stood up and prowled through the room, his hands thrust into his pockets—a tall, commanding, half-naked figure who looked as though he belonged to myth and not reality.

'I don't deal in hypotheses,' he said finally, stopping at the foot of the bed and staring at her intently.

'We can't pretend that it's not a possibility. You always tell me that I don't like facing unpleasantness, and I suppose you're right. I haven't got your strength.'

'You underestimate yourself.'

'Do I?' She smiled sadly. 'I don't think so. I feel as though I'm growing up at long last. As though I've spent my life inside a cocoon, and now I'm slowly having to break out of it.'

'You make that sound like a tragic inevitability,' he said, returning to sit on the bed next to her once again. 'There's nothing wrong with living in a cocoon.'

'Don't humour me, Oliver.'

'When I was young,' he said, 'I sometimes used to wonder what it would be like not to have to struggle for everything. I used to wonder about you sometimes.'

'About me?'

'You. I knew about you from my mother. I knew when you were born. I wondered what sort of life you led on the other side of the tracks.'

'A very different one from yours,' she said quietly. She wished that she had known him then. She wished that she could have been a fly on the wall and watched him as he grew from boy to man. Had he always had that supreme self-confidence, or had necessity given birth to it as he'd got older? A bit of both, she suspected. He had been born to succeed, with or without a moneyed background.

'We came from different worlds, Oliver, and that's where we must return. If the baby is lost there's nothing at all to keep us together.' She had to turn away when she said that because if she hadn't she would have burst into tears.

'You can have your freedom whatever happens,' he said abruptly, standing up again and walking restlessly across the floor, as though the energy in him couldn't be confined.

'I can?' There was no hope there in her voice, no exultation at this, what she had wanted all along, just despair at the thought that her freedom meant nothing to her without him near. He misread her question, though, because when he spoke his voice was cool but with an underlying savagery.

'Will you have a better rest now?' he asked, raking his fingers through his hair. 'Go to sleep, Francesca,' he said.

'We have to be at the hospital for nine, and that's less than four hours away. I'm going out for a swim.'

'A swim?'

'That's right.' His mouth twisted. 'You'll fall asleep quicker if I'm not in the bed next to you.'

'But you must be tired as well,' she protested, and he gave her a crooked, mirthless smile.

'You'd be surprised how easy it is to get used to having next to no sleep. I've spent my life working so hard that sleep is a pastime that I can usually take or leave.' He stood at the door and said as an afterthought, 'What were you doing while I was working my way up and doing without sleep?'

'Sleeping, I should think.'

He laughed and looked at her, and she thought for a split second that he was going to add something more, but he just said, 'I'll be back shortly. Get some rest.'

Then he was gone, and all semblance of laughter died from her face. She lay back against the pillows with her hands on her stomach and stared upwards at the ceiling.

There was the hurdle of the scan to get over, but all in all she decided that she should be feeling relieved. All that agonising over whether she had done the right thing in accepting his proposal of marriage, all that worry at the prospect of living with a man who didn't and couldn't return her love—it was gone now. She was free. She could return to England without the thought of that dark presence filling her life until she could stand it no longer.

But she wasn't relieved. She lay there, trying to imagine a life without Oliver Kemp in it, and she couldn't. It was as though he had embedded himself deep inside her—too deep for her to prise him out.

She finally drifted into a sleep of sorts, and was awakened by Oliver shaking her by her shoulder and telling her that it was time to get up. She hadn't heard him enter the room, but he must have been there for a while because he had showered and changed into a pair of trousers and a striped short-sleeved shirt.

'I must have a shower,' she told him.

'Be quick, then. The taxi arrives in fifteen minutes.'

So she hurriedly showered, noticing that she was still bleeding and already preparing herself mentally for what that meant. She wished that the hotel doctor, who had seemed so kind and efficient, was going to be there.

'Come on,' Oliver called through the door, and she hastily plaited her hair back and put on a light denim dress.

'Feeling better?' he asked as she joined him in the bedroom and grabbed her bag from the chair, and she shook her head.

'I'm dreading this,' she replied honestly. 'I'm not strong enough for this.'

'I'm strong enough for the both of us,' he murmured almost inaudibly, taking her hand and ushering her out of the room and out towards the taxi which was waiting downstairs.

When they arrived they found that the hospital was small, but they were efficiently shown through to the waiting room, by which time Francesca's nervousness was almost palpable.

There was a stack of outdated magazines on the table next to her, and she idly picked one up and began flicking through it, hardly seeing the print at all, very much aware of Oliver sitting next to her, and wondering what he was thinking.

The room was only half-full. Two heavily pregnant women sat opposite her, talking in their low, lilting accents, and next to them was a young girl who couldn't have been more than fifteen and who looked as though she should have been in school instead of in the maternity wing of a hospital.

When the doctor called her name Francesca automatically took Oliver's hand, which seemed to be waiting for her, and they went into the darkened cubicle.

'Relax,' the doctor told her. 'Legs flat on the bed, please. No need to be scared; this isn't going to hurt.'

He swivelled the machine round so that she and Oliver could both see it, and there it was. Fuzzy, tiny, but moving vigorously, and every single word the doctor said from then on was lost, because her whole mind seemed to have been taken over by the image on the screen in front of her. Her baby. Their baby.

'Looks fine,' the doctor said, not feeling the miracle that was unfolding underneath his blunt-headed instrument; it was just another scan in a morning full of them.

'I won't lose it?' she asked timidly, and he smiled at her for the first time.

'Shouldn't think so. But I'd try and stop throwing myself down steps, if I were you.'

Outside, fifteen minutes later, the sun was beating down. The taxi-driver had been instructed to wait, however long it took, and he was fanning himself with a newspaper, his windows rolled down.

Francesca looked around her. The world, she thought, was suddenly a wonderful place.

'Francesca,' Oliver said, once they were inside the taxi, 'we have to talk.'

CHAPTER TEN

BUT they didn't talk. Not inside the taxi. They travelled the distance in silence. Francesca stared out the window and saw the bright green trees, the bright blue sky, the picture-postcard prettiness of the scenery, but her thoughts were travelling round slowly in her head.

She knew what Oliver wanted to talk about—arrangements. They would have to discuss how the marriage was going to be annulled. She had no idea how one went about dissolving a marriage which had not even survived the honeymoon, but she didn't think that it would be difficult. A few forms to sign, perhaps, and then it would all be over barely before it had started.

Except, she thought, it had started long ago. It had started at the very moment that she had walked into that office—the very moment that she had set eyes on Oliver Kemp and something deep inside her had been ignited. And it would carry on too—long, long after a piece of paper told her that it no longer existed.

The taxi travelled slowly back to the hotel, and in the back seat of the car the distance between them seemed like a yawning chasm. Oliver was as preoccupied with his thoughts as she was with hers.

When the taxi-driver finally stopped outside the hotel and they got out she hovered indecisively by the car, waiting for Oliver, not knowing what she should do now.

'There's a bar overlooking the pool,' he said, not looking directly at her but taking her elbow, as though he thought that she might fall down without the support, although in fact she felt fine physically. The reassurance of the scan had given her a stamina that had not been there earlier on.

They walked to the bar, sat down at a small round table, and when their drinks had been brought to them she said in a rush, because she wanted to get it off her chest, 'I know what you want to discuss—arrangements for ending this and for visiting the baby once it's been born. Can't we leave it until we get back to England, though?'

It seemed horribly incongruous to be discussing things like that with the sun beating down, with lazy couples lounging by the pool, with the sound of the sea a distant, lapping noise, with birds flitting from flower to flower. The worst thing about beauty was that it made ugly things seem so much uglier.

Oliver didn't answer. He stood up, as though his restless energy needed some kind of release, and leaned against the veranda railing, staring down at the pool below. Then he turned to her, with his back against the railing, and said harshly, 'I'm not waiting until we get back to England. I can't.' His voice was flat and aggressive.

He had ordered a glass of fruit juice and he took a long sip, then carefully placed it on the table in front of him. She had ordered some variety of fruit cocktail, which had arrived complete with pieces of fruit, a miniature umbrella—the sort that children adored—and a cocktail stirrer, so she now stirred, staring down into the glass. She wished that he would sit down. When he loomed over her like that he made her nervous.

'Look,' he said abruptly, 'I can't talk here.' He picked up the glass again and drained the contents, and when she raised her eyes to his it was with more curiosity than nervousness.

There was something about his manner—something

edgy and slightly defensive which she couldn't quite put her finger on.

'But—' she began.

'Let's go for a walk on the beach.'

'In these shoes?'

She stuck one sandal-clad foot out and he snarled roughly, 'Leave the damn shoes by one of the tables on the beach.'

'There's no need to shout,' she snapped, standing up.

He muttered darkly, under his breath, 'Sometimes I think it's the only way to get through to you.'

'Thanks a lot! Any more compliments before we go?'

'I blame you,' he said almost inaudibly, moving off while she hurried to keep pace with his long strides. 'You always manage to turn me into someone I can hardly recognise.'

'So it's all my fault now, is it?' she threw at him. 'Will you stop running?' A couple who had been passing them from the beach to the hotel looked round at her tone of voice, and out of the corner of her eyes she saw the man smile—a sympathetic, amused smile that seemed to say, Women—aren't they always the same? Take them on an expensive holiday and they still manage to find something to shout about.

She lowered her voice and said, catching up with him, 'I'm not racing behind you on the beach. I don't see why we couldn't just stay at the bar and thrash this out, since you insist that it can't possibly wait until we get back to England.'

He didn't answer. He walked across to one of the umbrella-shaded beach tables and kicked off his shoes, then he rolled up his jeans a few times, stripped off his shirt and looked at her.

That, she thought, was another thing she wished he

wouldn't do—look at her. She could never get her thoughts straight when he focused those amazing light eyes on her. She removed her shoes, then walked alongside him with her hands clasped behind her back.

It was a very long beach. Just around the area of the bar, and by the sun-loungers, there were clumps of people lying on loungers or on towels on the sand, and a few in the water, but further along the beach was empty—an endless strip of unexplored white sand.

She wondered vaguely why people seemed to group themselves together on a beach when there was enough of it to spread themselves out, to lose themselves almost. Did they feel more secure if there were other people close by?

Oliver clearly did not believe in the group mentality. He was walking towards the far end of the beach, and she fell into step with him, unwilling to break the silence—not because she had nothing to say but because there was an absorbed tension in his body, in the tautness of his muscles.

'I told you that everything would be all right with the baby, didn't I?' he said, in an accusing, argumentative voice, and she looked at him from under her lashes.

'Why do you want to fight with me?' she asked. 'Do we have to? Can't we sort this all out in a civilised manner?'

'No, we cannot!'

They were far away now from the sun lizards, whose prostrate brown bodies were dots in the distance. He went across to a log and sat down, then he began doodling on the white sand with a thin twig.

It brought back a rush of memories for her—memories of a holiday in the sun with her father, when she had spent hours doing exactly the same thing—drawing on the sand, fascinated at the thought that everything she drew would be obliterated by the wash of the water.

Oliver, she suddenly thought, would make a wonderful father. She closed her mind to that anguished realisation and sat next to him on the log, prodding her toes into the warm sand and making a little mound like a molehill, which she promptly flattened only to start again.

'My father will be able to recommend a good lawyer...' she began, faltering.

'There will be no lawyer,' he bit out harshly, with his face averted from her.

'You mean that we'll do it all ourselves?' She frowned and looked across to him, and he met her eyes unwaveringly.

'I don't mean anything of the sort, Francesca,' he said grimly, and when she continued to stare at him uncomprehendingly he went on, 'Are you completely stupid? Do I have to spell it out for you? There will be no lawyer because there will be no divorce. Do you understand me now or do you want me to put it in writing?'

'But you said—'

'I know what I said! I'm not senile! But I've changed my mind. No divorce, Francesca.'

'Why? Because the baby is all right?' Tears stung the back of her eyes and she glared at him.

'Because,' he said, and a deep colour rose to his face, 'you belong to me and I have no intention of letting you go. Ever. Do you get my meaning? If you want a divorce, I'll fight you and you'll lose.'

'Why?' she whispered. 'Is it because Rupert took Imogen away from you? Is that it?'

He laughed—a harsh, grating sound. 'My God, woman. What Rupert and Imogen do is irrelevant.'

'Is it?' Francesca asked quietly. 'How can it be when you still love her?'

He shot her an incredulous look. 'Love her? Imogen? What I felt for Imogen might have been a hundred things, but it was never love.'

She felt as though someone had lifted her up and was swirling her around. 'Why were you planning to marry her, then?' she asked, dragging herself back down, reminding herself that the situation between them had hardly altered. 'Because you detested her?'

'Because,' he muttered, 'I was a fool—a blind, stupid fool who thought that fondness and superficial similarities provided sufficient grounds on which to base a lifelong commitment.' The challenge was there in his voice, as if he wanted her to dispute what he was saying so that he could argue with her.

How could she when she was too busy struggling to stifle the little seed of elation which was growing steadily inside her?

'And you think a baby provides those grounds?' she asked, and his voice, when he replied, was sober.

'No.'

The seed was rapidly growing into a plant. What was he trying to say to her now? It was as though wild hope was dragging her along to the answer, but before she could get there she kept bumping into an invisible wall which wouldn't allow her entry.

'What do you want me to say, Francesca?' he said tersely. He flung the twig away from him and she watched it scud across the sand to rest next to a coconut which had fallen from a tree. She felt a bit like that twig—whirling through space for a while before the inevitable bump back to earth. Reality was always just round the corner, she reminded herself sternly, waiting to trip you up.

For a while, once, when she had made love to him, when she had let her emotions dictate her responses, she had known what it was like to fly high above the clouds, but that hadn't lasted, had it?

'I just want you to make sense,' she told him.

'How can I make sense to you when I can't even make sense to myself?' he muttered. He stood up, stared out towards the sea, then sat back down, closer to her this time. 'You're hardly the type of woman I've been attracted to in the past,' he said roughly, and she went red with hurt anger.

'I know; you've already aired your thoughts on the subject!'

'You grew up in the lap of luxury. You've never known want or need or driving ambition. You've had life cushioned for you.'

'That was not my fault! I never asked to be brought into this world with a silver spoon in my mouth!'

'Oh, sure, you're a beautiful woman,' he went on, ignoring her. 'I can imagine that hundreds of men—boys, dammit, if that Thompson character is anything to go by— must have been enslaved by you.'

'Oh, thousands!' she snapped, knowing that she shouldn't let herself be rattled by what he was saying, or what he had said before in the past.

'But I thought I would be supremely immune to your brand of charm.' He looked at her then, and there was a savage fire in his eyes that sent a spark of flame leaping through her. She didn't dare say anything. It was as if time stood still, as if the earth had stopped revolving on its axis.

'I was wrong,' he said, catching her chin in his hand as though he was afraid that she might look away. 'When you started working for me I found myself stealing looks at you, and I told myself that it was because I needed to keep an eye on you, needed to see for myself whether you really lived up to the potential you'd displayed at that interview, but after a while I had to face the truth. I wanted to look at you because I was attracted to you. More every day.'

'You were?' Her eyes widened. 'You never showed it,' she whispered.

'I didn't want to admit it to myself, never mind admit it to you. I was engaged to a woman I thought was on my wavelength, then you walked into my life and suddenly nothing made sense any more. I kept telling myself that you weren't my kind of woman, but I was bewitched by you, Francesca.

'When I came round to your flat that night with the champagne it had nothing to do with being thoughtful. I just needed to see you, and then... God, when you invited me into your bed, when you undressed for me you were the most beautiful creature I had ever laid eyes on.' His face darkened at the memory and she felt a stab of pleasure course through her.

'You walked away,' she reminded him.

'I had to. You'd had too much to drink, but also I just needed to think, to try and sort out what the hell was happening to me. It was blessed relief when Imogen got herself involved with the Thompson fellow.'

She raised her hand and brushed his face with her fingers, and he caught her hand in his, opening it so that he could kiss her palm.

'I came back to you, and when I did I knew that I had to have you. I wanted you like I had never wanted anyone in my life before. I wanted to feel you against me; I wanted to possess you, body and mind. And just for an instant I thought that I had, but then everything started going wrong. I went abroad, and while I was there you started sounding cooler and cooler down the telephone, and it was driving me crazy.'

'I had no choice,' Francesca said quietly, even though there was a burning happiness inside her that made her want to grin and shout and laugh. 'I found out that I was pregnant. I also started thinking that the only reason you'd made love to me was because the woman you really wanted was no longer available.'

'How could you think that?' he asked. 'How could that even occur to you when it's you I love?'

Of course, she had guessed what he was saying in that roundabout, tortured fashion of his, but now his admission that he loved her spread through her like a fever, and she smiled and briefly closed her eyes.

'My darling,' she whispered, looking at him, her eyes bright. 'My darling Oliver. And I thought that I was suffering alone. Why do you think I started pulling back from you? Because I loved you; because I couldn't bear the thought that you would never return the feeling.'

He leaned forward and kissed her, his mouth hard and hungry, and she wrapped her arms around his neck, laughing as they rolled onto the sand. She traced the outline of his spine with her fingers and he groaned.

'You sent me to hell,' he murmured. 'I got back to a woman I thought I could tempt into my trap, only to find that she'd recognised the bait and was now running off in the opposite direction. When I realised that you were pregnant I also realised that the baby was my passport back to you. I made sure that you were married to me before you had time to think too hard about it, and I know that I used every legitimate trick in the book to get what I wanted.'

'Apology accepted,' she said happily, and he raised his feverish eyes to hers.

'Who's apologising? Tell me, Francesca; tell me that

you love me. Say it over and over again. It's your punishment for putting me through what I've been through.'

'I love you, Oliver Kemp,' she murmured obligingly, and she moaned as he pushed his hand under the opening of her dress to fondle the swell of her breasts.

'You don't know how I've longed to hear you say that. When you threw that accusation at me—that I'd hired Helen to take over from you behind your back—I could sense jealousy, and, God, how I wanted you to admit it, to tell me that you were madly jealous, because I would have been able to read what I wanted to in that.'

'I *was* jealous,' Francesca confessed. It seemed such a long time ago. 'I hated her when she said that she'd got my job.'

'Helen Scott will have to watch her step very carefully in the future,' he said grimly, then his features relaxed into a smile. 'Although she'll get her own due reward when my wife meets me at work to join me for lunch.'

'She'll hate that,' Francesca answered, but she felt so happy that it was impossible to harbour any bad feeling towards anyone.

'You can't imagine what I felt when I thought that you might lose the baby,' he said softly into her ear, 'when you told me that without the baby there was no need for a marriage.'

'You agreed!'

'Pride made me agree, but before the words were even out I knew that I couldn't let you go.'

She laughed with delight and he nudged her head back, kissing her neck, tugging open the remaining buttons on her dress so that he could expose an aching breast. His tongue flicked out and he licked the hard outline of her nipple, and she whimpered, wanting more.

'You're so different,' he said, looking up at her, and she

smiled at him—a dreamy, contented little smile; a smile
that no longer struggled to hide the love beneath it. 'The
more I saw you, the more I got to know you, and the more
I saw every one of those differences as a revelation. I had
no idea how grey my life had been until you came along;
then it was like having a blast of sun in a dark, shuttered
place. To start with I tried to ignore it, then I was suspicious, but eventually I couldn't hide from the truth. Life
without you is meaningless.'

'Good.' She sighed as his hand caressed her leg, her
stomach, her breasts.

How could she ever have thought that she would never
be happy? How could she have seen herself in a tunnel
without end? They said that the darkest hour was always
just before the dawn, but she would never have believed
that.

She looked at the tender, masculine face so close to hers,
and knew that from this perfect moment on the life that
was growing inside her would be born into love and happiness. The way it should be.

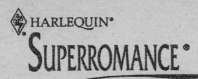

Romance is just one click away!

love scopes

- Find out all about your guy in the Men of the Zodiac area.
- Get your daily horoscope.
- Take a look at our Passionscopes, Lovescopes, Birthday Scopes and more!

join Heart-to-Heart,
our interactive community

- Talk with Harlequin authors!
- Meet other readers and chat with other members.
- Join the discussion forums and post messages on our message boards.

romantic ideas

- Get scrumptious meal ideas in the Romantic Recipes area!
- Check out the Daily Love Dose to get romantic ideas and suggestions.

Visit us online at

www.eHarlequin.com
on Women.com Networks